HERE WITH YOU

KELLY COLLINS

Copyright © 2022 by Kelley Maestas

No part of this publication may be reproduced, distributed, or transmitted in any form or by any means, including photocopying, recording, or other electronic or mechanical methods, without the prior written permission of the publisher, except as permitted by U.S. copyright law. For permission requests, contact kelly@authorkellycollins.com.

The story, all names, characters, and incidents portrayed in this production are fictitious. No identification with actual persons (living or deceased), places, buildings, and products is intended or should be inferred. All products or brand names are trademarks of their respective owners.

CHAPTER ONE

Emmaline Brown stared at the devil in front of her. Not the caricature type with flaming skin and a pitchfork, but the kind who wore perfectly fitting blue jeans and a T-shirt that read, *It's all fun and games until someone loses a wiener*. Miles McClintock set her life ablaze three decades ago and left it in ruin.

She kept a distance of about eight feet and circled him like a prizefighter. If she'd had gloves, she would've given him a right hook to that chiseled jaw, but a lady didn't ruin her manicure over a man.

"What are you doing here?" She looked past him to his truck, where a furry beast sat in the front seat. "And what is that?"

"That is not a what. He's a who, and his name is Ollie."

She stared at the dog, whose nose pressed to the glass, while his tongue lolled about. "There are no pets allowed at the resort."

He smiled and nodded toward her place. "Maybe not at The Brown, but The Kessler is allowing well-behaved dogs, and Ollie is the best."

She wanted to stomp her feet and scream, but she'd been raised better than to show such emotions. It was okay to broil inside until her organs were seared, but outside, she was as cool as shaved ice.

She gave the dog a final glance and turned her attention back to Miles. "Make sure he stays off Brown property."

"Duly noted." He moved forward a few feet, reducing her comfort level. "It's good to see you again, Emmaline."

The way he said her name made her grow weak in the knees, but she couldn't allow herself to go soft because of this man. "I go by Em." Miles was the only one who called her Emmaline. Even her parents, after a time, shortened her name to Em like everyone else. She was always in trouble and shouting Em instead of Emmaline saved time and stress on their vocal cords.

"I'll call you Emmaline."

She snorted and laughed. "Not if you want me to answer." A muffled woof came from the truck, but she ignored it. "Why are you here?"

"Your niece and nephew hired me to manage The Kessler."

"I know that, but why are you in town?" She always knew her meddling would bite her in the keister. When she faked the big C to get Brie to come home, she didn't know Carter was back in town. She intervened to get Brie to Willow Bay but had little to nothing to do with them falling back in love. That was the work of the universe righting a wrong. But … this was a complete betrayal. Not all failed first loves deserve a second chance. Especially not Miles McClintock.

"I was needed."

"The Kessler doesn't need you." Deep inside, she replaced the words with, "I don't need you." And she didn't.

She'd been fine the last thirty-odd years without him. "Besides, how does being an EMT qualify you to run a resort?"

It burned her bottom that he stood there, smiling at her like he was an equal. She'd been working at The Brown Resort since she popped out of her mama's belly. The truth was, she'd been running people ragged, but eventually, she caught on. She was born to do this, and if Miles thought he'd come in and change her life, he was wrong.

The Brown Resort was hers. Not by design but by default. She and the building that made up her family's legacy were connected in a way no one would understand. When people thought of The Brown, they thought of her and vice versa. She'd lost track of where the resort ended and she began. Now that Brie and Carter were married, that feeling bled into The Kessler.

"It doesn't qualify me, but that's where you come in." He looked over his shoulder as if hoping to find Brie and Carter driving back to save him. "They asked you to show me the ropes."

She'd love to show him a rope. One she'd toss over the willow tree and wrap around his lovely, corded neck.

When he turned back around, she could almost see defeat in his expression because Brie and Carter were nowhere in sight. They were off to Hawaii for their honeymoon. Just moments ago, they said goodbye and asked her to make Miles feel welcome. He was about as wanted as a murder hornet.

"Why here?" She knew exactly why. She was here, and he wanted to punish her. "Why are you back in town?"

He breathed in until his chest expanded, pulling at the cotton of his shirt until she was sure the fabric would tear.

He let his breath out with a sigh while she watched him deflate. "My mother is dying."

Her anger disappeared in an instant. When a person had nine toes inside heaven's gate, there was no room for petty squabbles. "I'm sorry, Miles, I didn't know." How was that possible? She had her finger on the pulse of everything and everyone in town. How did May McClintock's illness get by her? Then again, how did Miles coming back to town not get reported? *I banned my besties from ever talking about his family.* She hated it when her subconscious set her straight.

"It's cancer," he offered.

Her insides turned, twisted, and knotted themselves. She'd lied to her niece and told her she had the big C to get her to come home, and here was Miles, coming back to Willow Bay because his mother had it. Never in her life had she considered herself to be an awful person until that second. Well, there was that time thirty-something years ago when he told her what he'd done, and she left him. It wasn't one of her best moments, either. In her defense, she was young and under the influence of her parents. That shouldn't be held against her.

"I'm so sorry." May would have been her mother-in-law if things had worked out, but they hadn't. "Can I do anything?"

"For Mom, no, but you and I have unfinished business."

She glanced at her watch. "Wow, look at the time." She didn't have any place to be, but she couldn't stay there. "I need to go." Miles's presence did things to her insides that made her feel like she had the flu—light-headed, nauseous, feverish things. She needed to get away from him.

"You're leaving me?"

She swore he ended that sentence with the word

"again." It was written all over his face, even if he didn't say it.

"I can't babysit you. I have a life and important things to do." She waved her hand through the air like an orchestra conductor. "I'm sure you've got things to do, too. Don't you have a shift to pull for the town's ambulance service?" His being a recent addition as one of the town's EMTs was a blessing. At least that would give her eight hours a day where he wouldn't be underfoot. She didn't know what Brie and Carter were thinking, though. A resort manager needed to be on-site at all times. Well, she couldn't have it both ways, so this way was the best.

"No, I'm not employed by the hospital. The day Carter drowned, I was only helping fill in while I was in town, but I'm not a full-timer."

His words were both crushing and encouraging. Crushing because he would be around. But the words "while he was in town" alluded to him leaving, which meant this was temporary. She wanted to jump for joy but kept her happiness to herself. "You're leaving *again*?" She emphasized the word "again" because, ultimately, he had been the one who'd left town all those years ago.

To be fair, he had little choice. Once he'd turned his family in for fraud and lost everything, they'd disowned him. She broke off their engagement when he fell from grace, and her family no longer considered him a suitable mate.

"When I arrived, I didn't have a long-term plan. Since then, things have changed, and I'm sticking around."

Her heart sank. She could live in a world where Miles existed, but she didn't want him next door. He stepped closer, and she bolted for her car. "I've got to go."

"Do you have to, Emmaline, or are you abandoning me again?"

The way he said her name made her skin tingle. She once read cells had memories. Hers reflected on long days at the beach and longer nights in his arms. But how he said "again" erased that pleasant tingling, and shame danced across her skin. The feeling resembled ants—biting fire ants.

"I told you, I've got an appointment."

"Fine. When does my training begin?"

"Right now." She looked at the colorful beach towels and umbrellas dotting the sand. A toddler decked out in a life vest and arm floaties ran toward the water. Her mother dashed after her with a bottle of sunscreen in one hand and a sunflower hat in the other. "Don't talk to anyone. Don't be helpful because you aren't. And most importantly, don't be a pest."

"Basically, do nothing?"

"Exactly. Can you handle it?"

He shrugged, then grinned. "I can do that."

She got to her car and realized she couldn't pull off the ruse of having someplace to be if she didn't have her purse and keys, so she glanced at the mailbox. "Getting the mail, and then I'm out of here."

"You do you," he said. "Ollie and I will have a nice day on the beach. He loves the water." He started toward his truck.

"Dogs aren't allowed on the beach."

"That's not what my boss said. Carter told me to enjoy the facilities. Don't forget, Ollie behaves. He listens so well, he's almost human."

She frowned and placed her fists on her hips. "Since I've subleased the property and my staff is running it, I imagine that makes me the boss, and I say no dogs on the beach." She closed her eyes for a second and imagined Ollie digging holes and doing other unpleasant things.

He shook his head. "That makes you a renter, and I would imagine, as the manager, hired by the property owner, I have the last word." Ollie barked again, and Miles moved to the truck and opened the door. The dog leaped out and dashed straight for her.

Em had nothing to brace herself against when the dog jumped up and knocked her over. She lay flat on her back on the gravel driveway while the dog licked her face like she was melted ice cream.

"Get off!" She wriggled and squirmed, but the dog was relentless. She turned her head to see Miles's grin and knew he was enjoying this. "Can you make him behave?"

Miles let out a quick whistle and yelled, "Sit," and the dog did—on her legs.

"That's not helping." She attempted to roll him off, but he was all muscle, and no matter what she did, he wouldn't budge.

Miles walked forward and scratched the dog's ear. "Now that I have your attention, maybe we should clarify the rules."

"We know the rules. Carter and Brie asked me to train you. That puts me in the power position."

Miles looked down and chuckled. "Are you feeling powerful right now?"

She let out a huff. "No, I'm feeling nothing below my waist. He's cutting off the circulation to my legs."

Miles patted his leg, and Ollie jumped off.

She scrambled to her feet and pointed at the dog. "You call that well-behaved? I've seen smarter fish."

He leaned down and put his face close to Ollie's. "Don't you pay any attention to her." The dog wagged his tail and spun in a circle. "Yes, you're a good boy." Miles looked up and stared at her. "Don't you have someplace to be?"

Her head snapped back. She was momentarily left stunned and speechless. Momentarily, because lots of words came rushing back, but none she could spit out in public. Families and children were milling about. If she blurted out the expletives that danced on her tongue, she'd ruin the resort's reputation as family friendly. What she had to say to Miles would blister ears.

"I do." She started toward her house.

"I thought you were getting the mail?"

She couldn't think around him. "I must have gotten a brain injury from the dog attack."

Miles laughed. "Ollie is like me. He's a lover, not a fighter. Do you remember all those nights, Emmaline?"

She remembered them all right, and just the mention of Miles being a lover made her entire body vibrate with need. Damn memory cells. She marched to the mailbox, and when she opened it and found it empty, she stomped back toward him.

"Don't get comfortable because you're not staying."

"You're not the boss. I work for Brie and Carter. They said you'd be difficult."

She gasped. "I'm not." Standing in front of him, she pulled her shoulders back and hoped whatever height she gained would intimidate him enough to leave. Instead, he stayed there with a smug grin on his face. She needed a new tactic, and her southern sass came out. "Bless your little ole heart. You must have forgotten how things run around here."

He leaned in close until his lips were near her ear. "I know how you think things run, but your life is about to change, sweetheart."

"We'll see about that." Spinning around, she headed toward her house to get her keys and purse. She hadn't intended to go anywhere, but desperate times called for desperate measures. She needed reinforcements, so she texted 911 to her besties, the Fireflies, and told them to meet her at the diner. When she returned to her car, she dialed Brie, hoping to talk some sense into her.

Brie answered. "He's staying, Aunt Em, so don't try to change that. Besides, you promised you would help."

She did but under duress. When she offered to help, she wasn't expecting Miles McClintock to arrive. "He's not helping."

"Have you given him a chance?"

CHAPTER TWO

He knew this wouldn't be easy. Nothing with Emmaline was ever a walk in the park, but she was always worth it. He reached into the back of his truck and grabbed his duffle bag. He brought little with him when he got the call about his mom, but a man like him didn't need much.

"Come on, boy. Let's see what we're up against." He pulled the keys from his pocket and walked around the corner of the resort to where Carter said the house was. A small porch greeted him with a swing. On it was a pillow that said "Welcome," which made him laugh because he was anything but.

He opened the door and moved aside to let Ollie in first. The dog moved around the small living room, sniffing at everything. "What do you smell?"

Ollie looked at him as if he understood the question and shook his head. Carter told him to take the room down the hallway to the right, so he walked in that direction. The hardwood floor was lined with boxes of pictures. From the nail holes on the walls, he assumed they'd come from there.

He hadn't known the Kesslers well, but he knew the history between their family and the Browns. It was one-upmanship from the beginning. If the Kesslers got a boathouse, the Browns built a bigger one. If the Browns got new loungers, the Kesslers bought an upgraded model. Both families used their kids as pawns in their games.

He turned right into what would be his room. There was a full-size bed and a dresser, but not much else. The paint was faded where pictures had hung in the same place for years. Part of his job, while Carter and Brie were gone, was to paint the interior. He wasn't a fan of painting and could hire a crew, but that would draw attention to something he wanted to keep hidden. He was filthy rich.

Ollie sniffed the room's perimeter before jumping on the bed and curling up on the pillow.

"Make yourself at home." He dropped his duffel in the corner and went out the door to explore the rest of the place: a small eat-in kitchen and another bathroom. He didn't enter the master bedroom because it wasn't his space. However, it might be if the newest Kessler residents sold the resort to him.

His phone rang, and Cormac's face popped up on his screen. His nephew was the only good thing about his brother. How he raised such a great young man was a mystery. It probably had more to do with his former sister-in-law than with Darryl.

"Hey kid, what's up?"

"I'm in the parking lot and don't know where to go."

"Parking lot?"

"Of The Kessler? I stopped by the diner, and Cricket said you were moving in to take over. Why didn't you tell me?"

"I'll be right out."

He whistled, and Ollie came bounding down the hallway. "Cormac's here, buddy. Let's go play."

He walked out and around the building to find his nephew looking like he didn't belong. He hated that Cormac felt out of place.

He waved his arm in the air, drawing his attention. "Over here."

Cormac jogged to him. "This is great. How can you afford this?"

Telling Cormac he was interested in buying The Kessler was a major mistake he'd have to rectify. It made him look like he had the money to pay for it. A property like this had to go for millions. He hadn't told his nephew that he was the one who walked into the Five and Dime and bought the winning lotto ticket. Nobody knew the identity of the winner because he asked to remain anonymous. A lot was riding on him keeping that information close to his chest.

"I can't, which is why I took on the job as the manager."

Cormac's eyes widened. "You're going to manage this resort? Do you know how?"

"Nope, but I'll learn." Decades ago, he'd done the right thing for the right reasons, and everything turned out wrong. But there were great lessons learned in the process. "You can do anything you put your mind to. You can have anything if you work hard enough." *Or win the lottery.* "You want to chill on the beach for a while?"

"I don't have trunks."

Miles didn't either, but he had an idea. "Let's go." He walked up the steps of the screened-in porch and entered the lobby, where a dark-haired woman looked up and smiled.

"Welcome to The Kessler. I'm Margot. How can I assist

you today?"

Cormac stopped about two feet inside the door. "Margot Kincaid?"

She moved from behind the counter and ran to him. "Cormac McClintock. Look at you." She gripped his arms and felt his muscles. "What happened to the skinny little bean pole the football team tied to the goal posts?"

Miles watched his nephew's face grow redder by the minute. Cormac's eyes shifted right and left like he was looking for an escape, but Margot had him pinned in place with her hands massaging his biceps.

"I grew up."

"Yes, you did. You turned into a fine-looking man." She let her hands trail down his arms until she locked hands with him.

If Miles had walked in on them, he would have thought them a couple with how she stared at his nephew, like he hung the moon and a few stars, too. It was a good thing he'd gotten the lowdown from Carter and Brie about the staff at The Kessler. Margot was looking for a husband and someone to support her three kids.

"He doesn't have any money, Margot."

She dropped his hands and sighed. "The cute ones rarely do." She moved back to the desk. "Can I help you with something?" It was like a lightbulb went off as soon as she said it. "Oh, my gosh, you have to be Miles." She eyed him for a moment. "The hot cowboy who dated Em. People's descriptions haven't done you justice." Her hand went to her mouth. "This should be exciting. Does Em know you're here?"

"She does." He walked toward her. "Do *you* know why I'm here?"

She crossed her arms. "To manage The Kessler and

make sure I behave." She let out a phlegmy-sounding growl. "I could manage this place. I don't see why they didn't offer me the job as general manager instead of you."

Cormac laughed. "Because you molest the customers as they enter."

She smiled. "Only the ones with potential." She pulled a stack of towels from under the counter and folded the top one. "What do you need?"

"Swim trunks. Do you have a lost and found?"

She pointed to the door on the wall behind her. "Everything you could ever want is in there, from sunglasses to condoms." She smiled and added, "Unused."

A shiver went down his spine at the thought of wearing used condoms. "All we need is swim trunks."

She smiled. "It's like a swimwear shopping center. I found a designer bikini, but don't worry, I didn't take it. It has to be unclaimed for ninety days before it's up for grabs, but I've got my eye on it."

"Good to know." He didn't want to break any rules, so it was good he had some guidelines. "Let's go shopping." He and Cormac entered the storeroom. On one side were supplies like shampoo and bars of soap, and on the other were several boxes with months written on stickers on the sides of the bins. He found one dated September of the previous year and opened it. Margot was right. There was everything from a single rainbow sock to a frying pan. In the mix, he found four pairs of swimming trunks: two medium, one large, and one without a size. He took the two mediums and put the lid on the box. Ollie nudged his leg. "Sorry, buddy. I forgot you were here." He re-opened the box and dug through it until he found Ollie's favorite thing—a left shoe. He didn't know why, but his dog never touched the right shoes. "Shall we hit the beach?"

Cormac grinned. "I think I'll enjoy having my uncle run a resort. It comes with perks. You think I could bring my girl here sometime?"

Miles's eyes widened. "You got a girl?"

Cormac lowered his head and shuffled his feet. "In my head, she's mine, but she doesn't know it yet."

That boy was definitely his kin. Emmaline was his, too. Only, she hadn't been informed. He made a mistake over thirty years ago. He'd caught his father, the cattle marshal, falsifying documents to sell their cattle for a premium price. He'd always believed the ranch should run with honesty and integrity. He didn't know what the fallout would be when he confronted him, but he didn't consider complete devastation. In the end, his family lost all their wealth and disowned him. When he had nothing but his love to offer Emmaline, he lost her, too.

For years, he was bitter and angry. He walked away, promising never to look back. He thought he was over her until he returned to town. She showed up at the hospital the night Carter drowned, and all those old feelings surfaced.

"Did you get all your stuff from the preacher's house?"

"I didn't have much." The mention of the preacher brought him back to thoughts of Emmaline. He stifled a chuckle. She hadn't changed, and he knew exactly where she was going. She was stressed and needed her friends, who included Charlotte and Marybeth, the preacher's wife. They called themselves the Fireflies because they said they lit up a dark world, but most people knew what they really were: pretty little pests. Wouldn't Emmaline be surprised to learn he'd been staying in the guest house of one of her best friends? As the preacher's wife, it was hard for Marybeth to turn her back on one of her flock. Oh, to be a fly on the wall when that conversation happened.

CHAPTER THREE

E m walked inside the diner looking for her friends, but no one had arrived. It didn't surprise her since she called them before leaving the resort and then drove twice the speed limit to get to Cricket's.

She weaved through several tables to get to the empty booth in the corner. Cricket's Diner was the source of all gossip in Willow Bay, and Em didn't want to be tonight's news. Discussing delicate information here was like standing on a stage with a megaphone. The corner booth at least gave her some privacy. She slid onto the bench and inched herself into the corner before picking up a menu.

"Look what the cat dragged in." Cricket walked over and flopped onto the booth bench across from her. "You only come here when you need my honey or my advice. Which is it today?"

Em looked at the art above the booth. It was a picture of four chickens standing side by side with the caption, "What a fuster cluck." She had to agree.

"I need pecan pie and a quart of ice cream, please."

Cricket laughed so loud that everyone in the diner

looked their way. "The last time I served a bucket of ice cream, you were present, but you weren't the one partaking. Brie polished off that serving of diabetes in one sitting. If I recall, it was over a meddling aunt and a man who was back in town." Cricket kicked her feet up, and they landed right next to Em. "Seems to me that history might be repeating itself." Her red high-tops still had a middle finger drawn on the sole.

"Are you flipping me off, or are your feet tired?"

Cricket chuckled. "Oh, honey. If I were flipping you off, you'd know it. I've been here since five, and my dogs are tired."

Em took another look at Cricket's shoes. "You should get some shoes with support."

Cricket lifted a single brow. "Have you seen the shoes that have support? They go with compression socks and walkers." She wiggled her feet. "At least these are cute."

Em wouldn't call them cute—maybe if she were a teen. Then again, Cricket never seemed to age, so perhaps they were the shoes she wore back when.

The door opened, and Marybeth and Charlotte walked inside. Cricket looked over her shoulder and rose from the booth. "Looks like your posse is here. Do you want the whole pie?"

Em nodded. "And an order of fried pickles."

"If you get those pickles with ice cream, people will start talking and pregnancy rumors will race through town." Cricket leaned in. "It's not impossible, you know. There was a seventy-year-old woman in India who gave birth recently."

"Can you imagine?" Em asked.

Cricket laughed. "I'd rather poke my eye out."

"Me too." She looked around the diner at the townsfolk who were already eating up the fact that she was there and the other Fireflies were present. The only one missing was Tilly, but that was because she stayed back to run the kitchen. "But you're right. Wait ten minutes and then set them in front of Charlotte."

Her friends sauntered over. Marybeth looked out of place in the diner with her designer dress, her Kate Spade handbag, and her priced-for-the-runway shoes. Charlotte, as always, looked pageant-ready with her perfect makeup, not a hair out of place, and her ready-for-the-crown smile on her face. They slid into the booth Cricket had vacated only seconds before.

Cricket looked at them. "You girls want something, or is the gallon of ice cream and whole pecan pie going to do it for you too?" She wrote the order down and looked at Charlotte. "You've got an order of fried pickles coming up in ten."

"But I didn't—"

Cricket made a zip motion to her lips. "Yes, you did. Don't argue with your elders."

Charlotte nodded. "Yes, ma'am."

Their parents raised them with the same philosophy. You respect your elders and mind your manners. Em couldn't count the times her mother told her that good manners were free, but forgetting them would cost her dearly. Cricket was an elder, and she had earned their respect. Charlotte knew if Cricket said she was getting fried pickles, they'd show up as promised, and she'd smile and say thank you.

"Do you all want coffee?" Cricket leaned in. "I can put a shot of bourbon in it if it's one of those meetings." She turned toward Em. "Given that Miles showed up on your doorstep this afternoon to take over The Kessler, I think it's one of those meetings." She leaned back and held up her hand. "But if you're plotting murder, I don't want to be a part of it."

Em held up three fingers. "Coffee for all, and no side of bourbon or homicide."

Cricket left, and Em looked first at Charlotte and then at Marybeth before she started. "Why didn't anyone tell me?" She was referring to Brie and Carter making him the manager of The Kessler, but when she saw Marybeth's face pale, her heart skipped a beat. "You knew?"

"Well," she said in a voice that rose an octave. "How was I supposed to tell you Miles was staying in the church's guest house when I'm banned from saying his name?"

Em's stomach twisted. "Wait. What?"

"I said—"

"Oh, I heard what you said. The problem is, I can't believe it. How do you invite the devil inside your home, which happens to be the church, and live with yourself?"

"Everyone is redeemable—even Miles."

"Are you kidding? That's like inviting a fox into the henhouse or putting a snake inside a hamster habitat." She realized she was yelling when she looked around, and all eyes were on her. She leaned in and whispered, "What kind of friend are you? You opened up Heaven and invited Hades inside. Who does that?"

Marybeth sat taller and smoothed the lapel of her Chanel jacket. She dressed for an event every day, and right now, Em second-guessed her promise to Cricket to pass on murder.

"I'm the friend who honors your wishes and still does the right thing. His mama is dying, and that SOB of a brother won't let him stay on the ranch. With the resorts all full for summer, I couldn't let him sleep in his truck, which was where I found him. One night, he'd pulled into the church parking lot and parked under that big elm." She tugged at her pearl necklace. "As far as who does that? Don't forget that Jesus forgave Judas."

Em couldn't argue with a preacher's wife. She stared at both of her besties, then turned her attention to Charlotte. "Did you know?"

Charlotte tilted her head to the side and opened her mouth to speak but immediately shut it. She waited the longest of seconds before she said a word. "Can I plead the fifth here?"

"Oh. My. God."

Marybeth brought her hand to her heart. "I'll pray for you."

Em shook her head. "Nope, you better pray for yourself. At the very least, pray that my ice cream and pie get here soon." She pushed all the knives toward Charlotte. "You better hide these before I decide to use them."

Charlotte cleared the table of anything Em could use in a murder, including blunt force instruments like the sugar jar. She picked up the forks and analyzed them carefully before setting them down.

"I could fork you to death," Em said.

Charlotte smiled. "You could, but you're getting pie, and you were never one to mix sweets and protein." She slowly pushed a fork to Em. "Now that murder is off the table, or at least the weapons, can we get to the good stuff?"

"There is no good part." Em leaned back against the booth and groaned. "Why am I being punished?"

Marybeth reached across the table and took Em's hand. "You're not being punished. You're being tested."

Em closed her eyes and scrubbed her face. "That's even worse. With Miles, I've got a failing score."

Charlotte tidied their napkins and placed the forks in

the center. When she looked up, she frowned. "Is that what you were wearing when he showed up?"

Em looked down at her shirt and jeans. It was laundry day at the resort, and these were her cleaning clothes. "I wasn't expecting company."

"Did your mama drop you on your head when you were a child?" Charlotte asked. "You always dress for success. Right now, you look like you went from debutant to disaster."

"It's laundry day." Em pointed to each of them. "I still can't believe you didn't warn me."

Marybeth looked to the ceiling like she was praying for a godly intervention, but none was coming. "What were we supposed to do? Call anonymously and say, 'He-Who-Must-Not-Be-Named is on his way?'"

"That would have worked."

Charlotte laughed. "This isn't *Harry Potter*."

Em let out an exasperated sigh. "No, this is real life. My life. And you two are meddling."

"Wait a minute," Marybeth said. "All I've done is be neighborly."

Charlotte raised her hand. "And all I've done is follow your rules."

Cricket came by with the tub of ice cream and a whole pecan pie. "The rumors are spreading. So far, we've got one table speculating that you tried to hook up with Miles again, and he turned you down. Two tables bet that you read the travel article in today's Gazette about the critic coming to Willow Bay, and you're afraid The Brown isn't up to snuff."

"Excuse me?" Em's jaw dropped. She should have been appalled that anyone would think she couldn't hook up with Miles McClintock again, but what shocked her the most was the news about the travel critic, or that anyone would think The Brown isn't up to snuff. "Someone is coming to The Brown?" She knew many travel critics by name and tried to remember the guests visiting in the next few weeks. No one stood out. "Do you have the paper?"

"It ain't free," Cricket said.

"Add it to the tab, then split it between those two." She pointed at Marybeth and Charlotte. "They owe me."

Cricket walked away, and Em smiled. This was a great distraction. "Can you believe a travel critic is finally coming to Willow Bay?" Her family had been waiting for a lifetime to be written up as the best place to stay in Texas, but their little town was a dot on the map and grabbed little attention. The critics focused on areas like the California wine country or bed and breakfasts in Vermont. "I can't believe it. I finally have a chance to make my family proud."

Her friends stared at her like she was one of these screaming goats she always saw on the internet.

Marybeth gave her a pitiful look. It was the kind she gave to a parishioner at a funeral—an I'm-sorry-for-your-loss-expression. "Have you lost your ever-lovin' mind? Honey, no one in your family is here to see it."

"Maybe they're in heaven looking down at me?"

"Honey, we're talking about your family here." Marybeth didn't need to elaborate. Her family wasn't known for their pious behavior.

"I'm here, and it's important to me."

Charlotte picked up a fork and dug into the pie. "I'm with Marybeth on this."

Cricket dropped off the paper, and under Trixie's Travels, she found the article and read it twice.

"It says a famous travel critic will come in the next few weeks to see what Willow Bay has to offer."

"It doesn't say they're staying at The Brown," Charlotte said. "We're a tourist town with lots of options."

Em blew air through closed lips and waved that notion away with a brush of her hand. "There's only one option, and that's The Brown Resort. Everything else is substandard."

"Don't forget about The Kessler. Your family tried to dismiss them for decades, and you see how that worked out?" Charlotte frowned. "Did you meet Miles looking like that? You don't even have any makeup on."

Em didn't want to talk about Miles or makeup. Something big and exciting was coming her way. "What does it matter? I'm not looking to impress Miles, but if you must know, I was made up. Ollie licked it off."

"Who's Ollie?" Charlotte asked.

Though she acted irritated about the dog earlier, in hindsight, she had to admit the entire situation was funny. "Miles's dog."

"Cute little bugger," Marybeth commented.

Em rolled her eyes. "He's one of those furry yellow ones that probably drools as much as he farts." She covered her mouth to quiet her laugh. "He attacked me."

"And you're laughing?" Charlotte asked.

Em shrugged. "Yes, because Miles claimed he was well-behaved. It just shows you what a poor judge of character the man is."

Marybeth looked at her with a pinched expression. "Don't forget he once chose you."

"And you chose him until you chose your family and that stupid resort instead," Charlotte added.

Em jammed her spoon into the ice cream. If they were going to revisit old hurts, she'd need sugar. Before responding, she ate two heaping spoons of ice cream and three bites of pie. "I didn't have a choice. He screwed up everything. Who does that?"

"A man with integrity," Marybeth answered. "He risked everything so you wouldn't join a family who was as dirty as the soles of their boots. And you left him when they disowned him because he no longer had his family's fortune to offer."

She knew that's what everyone in town thought, but it wasn't the whole truth. She was a Brown and was raised with one rule that trumped all others. You did what your daddy said, and her daddy forbid her to marry Miles after that catastrophe. If she'd left with him, her father would have disowned her. Would that have served any of them well?

"Did you even really love him?" Charlotte asked. "He asked you to go away with him."

"Of course, I loved him. But you'll never understand my life." She eyed Marybeth. "Your daddy was a preacher, and his daddy was a preacher, and you were raised on faith, hope and forgiveness." She turned to look at Charlotte. "And your parents ran the summer camps, so you were raised on kumbaya, and s'mores. My Daddy was like J. R. Ewing. His power surpassed the family. No one messed with J. R.. Hell, no one breathed without his permission."

Charlotte smiled. "Not until someone shot him." She tapped her chin. "I learned how to shoot at summer camp and was a pretty good shot. I might have been able to help."

Even then they were thick as thieves, and she was pretty sure Charlotte would have taken that shot for her. "Are we talking about murder? Daddy's long gone and dead."

"True," Marybeth said. "Let the dead rest and stop living by their rules."

She didn't want to point out that Jesus had been gone

for thousands of years, and they still lived by his rules. There were some battles she'd fight, and other's she'd let go, and that was one of them.

As she thought about the day Miles left, old feelings churned inside her. People expected her to break down after the breakup, and she did, but never in public. She was southern born and raised. By day, she appeared unphased because that was how the Browns did things, but she cried into her pillow every night for a year.

"Where would we have gone, and what would we have done? If I had left with him, we would have been sleeping under that big elm tree in your parking lot years ago. I made the best decision given the circumstances."

"Now that he's back, and you don't have your daddy to make the rules, what will you do this time?"

"This time is different because he's not asking me to leave with him." Em smiled. "Besides, I don't have time for Miles. I have to get ready for the critic."

Marybeth sighed heavily, and Charlotte forked another bite of pie.

"When will you learn that the resort will never appreciate or love you back? It doesn't rub your feet at the end of a long day or hug you when things are tough. Those bungalows your family put in aren't the same as toe-curling kisses," Marybeth said. "And that boathouse you built to keep up with the Kesslers won't give you earth-shattering orgasms."

Em held up her hand. "Not true. Some of the best sex I've ever had was in that boathouse."

Both of her friends smiled as if they'd made their point, and they had. It wasn't the boathouse that tickled her bits to perfection but stolen moments there with Miles. What was she going to do about him?

CHAPTER FOUR

Dressed in borrowed swim trunks, Miles led the way to the beach. "Stay on The Kessler property." He nodded toward The Brown Resort. "Little Miss Sunshine next door doesn't want the riffraff mingling with her guests." He glanced at Ollie. "You stay away from people's shoes." The leather sandal he found in the box hung from Ollie's mouth. "That's all you get for the day." Ollie didn't chew his treasures. He carried them around with pride and showed them to anyone who'd pay attention. "Ollie has a shoe fetish I can't seem to break, so keep yours where you can see them. Once he disappears with them, they're often gone for good." He didn't know where they went, but they'd sometimes show up months later to be loved and appreciated again.

"Does he eat them?"

"I've never seen him chew one, so I don't think so, but that doesn't mean he doesn't swallow them whole." He found two empty lounge chairs by the water's edge and tossed their towels on them to stake a claim. "I imagine they'd be hard to digest. I think he buries them."

All around them, guests laughed and played in the water. Though he felt guilty for not working, he was following directions. Emmaline told him to do nothing. Sunning himself at the water's edge was as close to doing nothing as he could manage.

Cormac opened one of the two beers he'd taken from the refrigerator and handed Miles one. "This is the life." He laid back on the lounger facing the water. "Do you get to do this every day?"

Miles took his seat and gulped his beer. "I imagine not, but it's a nice way to enjoy an afternoon." He'd spent most of his life working and not much time playing. When he left Willow Bay, he went to school to be a paramedic. He figured he'd ruined enough lives by exposing the truth. He'd make up for the hardships he'd caused by saving lives. The problem was that not everyone wanted or could be saved, and the losses piled on him like heavy weights, leaving him wanting a career change. While unexpected, an offer to try managing the resort before he bought it was exactly the change he needed. "What have you been up to?"

"Since my dad kicked you off the ranch?"

He took another gulp to douse the fire that burned in his heart. "He didn't kick me off the ranch. He can't do that as he doesn't own the ranch. It belongs to your grandmother. He asked me to leave, and I did because I don't want to cause trouble."

"You know my dad will inherit it when Granny May dies, right?"

He imagined that was true since he'd been disowned decades ago. Most would feel bitter about that, but the ranch was run down and wasn't worth much. The only thing of value was the land. There was so much that could be done with the property, but his brother Darryl wasn't a visionary and settled for raising chickens and a few cattle he sold to the locals.

"How is your grandma?" He visited her first thing when he came to town. May McClintock had always been a sturdy woman, but he barely recognized her. Cancer had eaten her alive; she was as thin and fragile as a flower.

"She's hanging in there. She keeps asking when you're coming back to see her."

"I need to work on that." With his brother unhappy about his return, it wouldn't be easy, but nothing was impossible. He'd survived worse. Long ago, his family had tossed his belongings in the back of his truck and escorted him off the ranch. He could still see his mother standing on the porch with tears in her eyes. Despite her sadness, she'd never reached out to him. He hadn't heard from anyone except Cormac, who called to tell him his father had died. That's how they started a relationship.

"I'm glad you tracked me down all those years ago." His dad died nearly five years ago from a heart attack. Cormac found Miles on social media and reached out to tell him the news.

"You had a right to know." He stared off toward the ocean. "I wish you could have come to the funeral."

"I don't mind missing it. Lying in a casket is not how I want to remember him." Miles's fall from grace was not a family secret, so he didn't need to explain it again. Cormac had heard both sides. His father's version, where he'd taken a wealthy family and made them dirt poor, and Miles's, where he'd defended his decision to do the right thing. Since his nephew was sitting next to him drinking a beer, he imagined Cormac was a man who weighed the evidence and made his own choices.

"Were you really engaged to Em Brown?"

"Yes, I was." Miles took another drink and closed his eyes, picturing her years ago with her long honey hair and dazzling smile. She was beautiful then, and she was beautiful now. Emmaline was the rebel of the two Brown sisters, which was why he was sure she'd pack up and go with him the day he drove over to get her. But news in a small town traveled fast, beating him to The Brown. When he got there, she'd already been given her decision by her father. He was no longer an acceptable suitor. There was no way Horace Brown was allowing his dirty McClintock blood to enter the Brown family tree. He brushed away thoughts of the past and focused on the here and now. "Tell me about this girl who's yours but doesn't know it."

Cormac sat up and smiled. "Tiff."

He turned to his nephew with both brows raised. "Who?"

"Tiffany Townsend. She owns the candy store. You know, the one with the taffy-pulling machine in the window."

"And you're sweet on her."

He patted his stomach. "I've gained ten pounds since spring from visiting that place."

"You ever ask her out?"

He shook his head. "She's got a kid, and her ex keeps showing up. I don't want to start something if she's still got one foot in the door with him."

"Have you asked her about him?"

Cormac looked horrified by the idea. "Hell, no. I don't want to know anything about him."

He chuckled. "Yes, you do. You want to know if he's in or out of her life."

"I can't just walk in and ask. Besides, word on the street says she's about to lose the store. I don't think it makes enough money to make ends meet. I suppose all will be decided after the tourist season ends. She's got enough on her plate to deal with. I don't need to add to her woes."

"Maybe you'd be an asset and not a woe. Your sweet tooth is contributing to the bottom line."

"I can't save the store on my small contribution, but I try to help. I'm going to take the wait-and-see approach. You can learn a lot by standing back and watching."

"You're a wise man, Cormac." He wanted to ask who he got that from because it wasn't from his father. Darryl wasn't the brains in the family. "Maybe she can get a rent reduction. Who owns the building?"

Cormac frowned. "Her ex for now. Cricket says he owns several storefronts on Main Street. He's not from here. She met him in Dallas. It would suck to answer to someone you're no longer with. I imagine they keep ending up together because she can't completely cut ties with him, having his kid and all."

He looked over his shoulder at The Brown Resort. "It's hard to work with your ex and stay emotionally detached." With less than one day under his belt at The Kessler, he second-guessed his decision to manage it.

When he came to town, he had no intention of staying. But seeing Emmaline made him want more than he had, and after his lotto win, he had a lot he wanted to share with her. Deep inside, he knew he could make things right. The problem was that he was torn about his approach. She'd never married, which either meant he'd ruined everything to do with love for her back then, or she'd never found someone who filled her heart as he had. The biggest issue was that she left him when he lost everything, so if they ever had a chance again, she couldn't know about his windfall. He didn't want money to be a factor a second time. If he and Emmaline were meant to be, she'd need to fall in love with him the way she saw him—a man with a dog and a truck and not much else.

"I wish there was something I could do to help her."

"I'm no expert on women. I crashed and burned the first time, but maybe just be her friend at first. The best relationships start as friendships." That's how he and Emmaline started. They were study buddies in high school, and that friendship grew into something more.

"Did you ever fall in love again?"

He could honestly say he hadn't. He hadn't been a celibate saint since they broke up, but he'd never let another woman in. His bed, yes, but not his heart. "Nope. Emmaline was the one for me. She was the perfect amount of sass and class to make me happy."

"Do you think you guys might have a second chance at it?"

He breathed deeply, inhaling the salty air mixed with sunscreen and hope. Logic said no, but he'd been working purely on instinct since he returned to town. Over the years, there'd been a little voice in his head that he used to ignore. The same voice told him not to turn his father in. It screamed at him to let the powers that be deal with it, but his future father-in-law was getting ready to put down a significant investment and partner with the McClintocks. Miles knew when it all went to hell, it would get ugly. Wasn't it better to blow things up before Horace lost a fortune and blamed him?

Over the years, he'd learned to listen to the voice. Had he listened to it years before, maybe things would have been different. He'd been listening closely now. It told him to buy a lotto ticket from the Five and Dime. It told him to take the shift the day Carter drowned. It told him to ask Cormac to set up a meeting to see if Carter wanted to sell his property. He wasn't sure what would happen between him and Emmaline, but he knew that voice in his head was telling him to stay put until he figured it out.

"That depends on where Emmaline's priorities are. She's married to the resort, and I'm unwilling to be a misteress to her job."

"Don't you wish you were rich?"

He hated holding back the truth from Cormac, but he had to. His newfound wealth complicated a lot of things. He had the cash to change many lives, but was it wise? He could rush in and save the ranch, which had turned from a thriving cattle ranch to a wasteland. And maybe he should since he was the one who financially destroyed it, but the voice in his head screamed, "No!" He had to keep reminding himself that he wasn't the one who'd been cheating people. The reckoning was already coming. He'd sped it up. When it came to Emmaline, he'd take Cormac's wait-and-see approach.

"Money isn't always the answer. Everyone thinks it is, but imagine if you were rich and Tiffany was in the same position of need. If you swooped in and saved her, and she started dating you, wouldn't you question her motives? Let her fall in love with you, not your money."

Cormac laughed. "That's easy. I don't have any."

"You want to earn some?"

Cormac sat up like Ollie did when a treat was involved. "Is The Kessler hiring?"

Miles shook his head, and his nephew's shoulders sagged. "Nope, but I am. Do you think you can bring your grandma over for dinner? I'll make a reservation at The Brown for tomorrow night. I also have some painting in the residence that needs to be completed before Brie and Carter return."

"I've always wanted to eat at The Brown. Am I invited to dinner, or am I simply the chauffeur?"

"Eating there is a perk of working for me." It was a brilliant plan that checked off many boxes. He needed to spend time with his mother. Cormac needed a job to keep him in candy, and dining at The Brown would put him in Emmaline's path.

Feeling good about his next move, he leaned back, drank the rest of his beer, and set the bottle in the sand before closing his eyes. A shadow fell across him a while later, and he opened his eyes to find Emmaline standing there with her arms crossed.

"Break time is over. You've got work to do." Her upper lip curled as she bent over to pick up his empty bottle. "Don't make drinking on the job a habit."

He sat up and stared at her. "You told me to do nothing." Something had changed in the time she'd been gone.

"Now I'm asking you to do something." She pointed to his bare chest. "Get dressed. We can't have you distracting the guests."

He glanced around and saw no one looking at them. "Maybe it's you I'm distracting."

"Don't be ridiculous. You annoy me, but I said I'd be nice and train you." She looked at her watch. He hadn't noticed earlier, but it was the watch he'd given her the Christmas before they split up. It was a simple gold watch with little diamond chips circling the face. It had little value, so she must have worn it for the emotional connection. It made him feel good that she kept a piece of him with her.

"If this is her being nice," Cormac said, "I'd hate to see her be mean."

Miles smiled and rose to his feet. "Oh, that's when the real fun starts." He grabbed his towel and wrapped it around his shoulders. "Enjoy the beach, Cormac. I'll see you tomorrow."

Ollie woofed and danced around Emmaline's legs, trying to get her to pay attention. "Can you control your beast?"

"He seems to like you."

"He has good taste." As he and Emmaline walked toward the resort, she pulled a list out of her back pocket and handed it to him. "Here's your to-do list for today." Menial tasks filled the front and back. The first item was scraping gum from the bottoms of the picnic tables.

"This is managerial work?"

She stopped in front of The Kessler. "You don't get to come back here and start at the top. You need to earn your way. You can't be a good manager if you don't understand the work others are expected to do." She turned and walked away.

He called after her. "How long will you punish me?"

CHAPTER FIVE

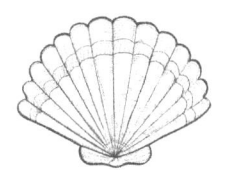

She left him in front of The Kessler and headed straight for Tilly and the kitchen. "Do you have any of those sticky buns from breakfast?"

"Didn't you just eat a quart of ice cream and a pecan pie for lunch?"

Em's jaw dropped. "How did you know?"

Tilly put on a fresh pot of coffee and walked to the little table by the window. "Cricket called, and then the girls phoned. They said you'd need to eat something healthy and fortifying; a sticky bun doesn't fall into that category."

"They have nuts, which are protein, and butter, which is dairy. That's healthy." Em flopped into the chair facing the window, which gave her a view of the garden walkway and The Kessler. Moments later, Miles appeared with his to-do list and a scraper. Did the man have any T-shirts that hung loose, or did they all fit him like a second skin?

Tilly poured two cups of coffee and joined her at the table. "They say what comes around goes around." She nodded toward Miles. "I'd say that's a delicious serving of karma."

"He may be yummy to look at, but you know what they say, too much is just too much."

Tilly pulled a sticky bun from a nearby rack, plated it, and handed it to Em. "True, but it doesn't stop you from indulging. My mom told me I didn't eat until I was full. I ate until I hated myself."

"Just looking at him gives me a toothache." She closed her eyes and massaged the bridge of her nose, praying he'd be gone when she opened her eyes, but nope, there he was, looking as decadent as one of Tilly's treats. "Can you believe he's here?" She lowered her head to the table and banged it on the wood several times. "I can't believe everyone kept this from me. He's working next door, for God's sake. And speaking of God, he was staying with Marybeth."

"Will you forgive the girls for not letting you know he was staying at the church?"

Tilly was the kindest soul she knew and fiercely loyal, which made her the best of friends. She arrived at The Brown years ago looking for a job and worked her way up from prep cook to executive chef.

To not forgive them would make her a hypocrite. "I told them never to mention his name. As far as I was concerned, Miles McClintock was dead to me."

She turned to look out the window. "What a resurrection. Have you seen those muscles?"

"I haven't noticed."

Tilly laughed. "You're a terrible liar."

Em took a bite of her sticky bun, but the sweetness made her stomach turn, so she set her fork on the plate, pushed it aside, and stared out the window.

"Why does he have to look so good?"

Tilly sipped her coffee. "Because karma is a bitch."

"He's out there looking like Adonis, and look at me. Even Charlotte thought I looked like roadkill." She brushed her hair back from her face. "That's because his damn dog licked my makeup off."

"That expensive stuff Charlotte brings you?"

She tried to remember what she'd put on that morning and giggled. "I suppose I can't blame him. I was wearing Cricket's honey on my crow's feet."

Tilly touched the crinkled corners of her eyes. "You don't have crow's feet. Yours are more like sparrow's feet." She thumbed the corners of her eyes. "Look at me. I have pelican claws."

Em stared at Tilly. The longer someone was around, the less you noticed them. Tilly had grown up with her. She was a sister from another mister, and she saw her every day, but she never noticed how she'd aged over the years. Now that she was paying attention, she saw the fine lines her friend described as pelican claws.

"You're crazy. You don't look a day over thirty."

"I already said it. You're a terrible liar." She reached for the honey on the table. "Do you think it works?"

"It can't hurt." She held up her hand and shook her head. "Scratch that. It can if you get it in your eyes." She'd done that once and had to visit Dr. Robinson for an eyewash.

They watched Miles continue to scrape off the gum from the underside of the picnic table. "Are you punishing him?"

She was a lousy liar and didn't want to be dishonest to Tilly or herself. "Partly." Then she remembered the news. She clapped her hands and jumped up and down in her seat. "Trixie posted today about a travel critic visiting

Willow Bay. Having an extra set of hands to do the dirty work could be more of a boon than a bother."

"They never said they were coming to The Brown." Tilly reached into the discarded paper basket and pulled out today's Gazette. She opened it to Trixie's Travels column and pointed. "Read it."

Em pushed it away. "I've already read it, but where else would they stay? When you're looking for luxury, you come to The Brown."

Tilly leaned back and crossed her arms. "There's The Kessler, and what about the campgrounds or Airbnb's?"

A bitter taste rose in Em's throat. Comparing The Brown to The Kessler or a campground was unthinkable. No rental home would be equal either.

"Have you lost your mind? The Kessler is barely open, and a campground? People have to pee in bushes and bathe in a stream. There's no air conditioning, rowboats, or room service. There's no Tilly and her fabulous Shepherd's Pie." She reached for her discarded plate. "And there aren't any hot-from-the-oven sticky buns in anyone's rental home."

"You got me there, but I don't think the critic is coming to give my buns a try." She stared out the window. "Speaking of buns. He wears his jeans well."

She didn't want to look but couldn't help herself. "That man needs a uniform."

Tilly smiled. "Speedo?"

That wasn't a vision she needed in her head. "No one wears Speedos these days."

With a shake of her head, Tilly said, "Not true. Do you remember when my Uncle Werner visited? He wore that one with the daisy right—"

"Don't remind me." Em covered her eyes. "I remember.

We had the housekeeper steal it when he was out, so no one else had to be subjected to that view."

"It's probably in lost and found. Maybe you can pull it out and ask Miles to wear it. You think he could rock that daisy?"

"You're torturing me, right?"

Tilly shrugged her shoulders. "It seems only fair since you're making him do stuff you wouldn't do."

"Not true. I've scraped plenty of gum."

Tilly laughed so hard that her staff stopped what they were doing. She was a stoic woman, so laughter was out of character. She turned and pointed at them, giving them a stern look. "Back to work." She returned her attention to Em. "The only gum you've scraped is what ends up on your shoe. Why are you being so harsh? It's been decades. Let it go."

"He ruined my life."

Tilly sipped her coffee and stared at Em. "You ruined your life when you refused to go with him."

"Seriously? It's not like I had a choice."

Tilly turned red from her neckline to the tips of her ears. "You always have a choice, and you chose the resort. Let me ask you this ... is it warming your bed at night? Does it hold your hand when you're sad?"

"Me? What about you? You're married to this resort, too."

Tilly stood. "No, ma'am, I'm not. I stay because of you. Don't forget, Edelweiss is my dream."

"That's the second time you've mentioned leaving. If you want to go, then go!"

"I stay because of you. Imagine this kitchen without this table and our talks. If I'm gone, they end." She pointed to Miles. "You had a future with him and let him down."

She couldn't believe her ears. "Miles screwed it all up."

"What's wrong with you Browns? One sister couldn't let go of the man she loved and ruined lives by keeping him. The other tossed the man who loved her aside. I'd have left with him if he'd been into short, stocky German women."

"He could be." She waved a dismissive hand. "He's all yours if you want him."

After a long, exaggerated sigh, Tilly hugged Em. "Stop lying to yourself. You never got over him. It's why you never married." She nodded to where Miles stood, pulling dead fronds from the palm trees. "He never married either. He's back because he's not over you."

"He's back in town because his mother's dying."

"He could have stayed at Marybeth's, but he's here. And I'm sure that has everything to do with you. So, Emmaline Brown, you've got a decision to make. Will you let him in, or will you chase him away like you did the last time?"

"That's not fair."

"Life's not just, but we keep living it. How will you live yours? You know, there's more to life than the resort."

"It's all I know."

"Oh, honey, it's all you've allowed yourself to know." She stared at Miles struggling to pull a dead frond free. "When was the last time you landscaped?"

"Okay, I'm punishing him, but he broke my heart."

"Imagine how he felt when he came to get you, and you sent him away." Em opened her mouth to defend her actions, but Tilly shook her head. "He did the right thing. He lost everything to be an honorable man. Put yourself in his place when you're alone, lying in bed tonight, and imagine what his life has been like. You lost him, but he lost every single thing in his life."

Tilly moved behind the stainless-steel prep counter and

looked at the orders. It was nearing dinnertime, and she was back to business, which meant Em was dismissed. She might own the resort, but Tilly was the queen of the kitchen.

As she made her way outside, she asked herself what it would take to forgive Miles. She'd had decades to think about it, so she marched over to him to get the answer to the question that had haunted her for years.

"We were supposed to get married. We were supposed to be partners. Why didn't you make me part of your decision?" Just asking released thirty years of fury. "Why did you ruin everything?"

CHAPTER SIX

He knew she had questions and deserved answers, so he put down the fronds and sat on the nearby picnic bench. Emmaline took the seat across from him as he looked at the waves lapping against the shore. The tiny whitecaps bubbled on the sand before they soaked in and disappeared. At least four or five cycles passed before he figured out what to say. "Every window has two views. You're either looking out or looking in."

She gathered her long hair on top of her head and somehow skewered it with a pen to stay in place. "I get that we see things through different lenses, but how can you not see what you did was wrong?"

He rubbed the scruff on his face. "You're right. I was wrong." He sat with one leg over each side of the bench and swung his outside leg inside to face her fully. This was the conversation they should have had thirty years ago, but they didn't have the maturity to put what they felt into words.

"I'm glad we agree on something."

"You made a choice, and I couldn't understand why you didn't choose me all those years ago, but I understand now." He scanned the beach, the bungalows, the main house, the restaurant, and the resort. "In life, there are always choices. Often you have to decide if you're going to support the devil you know or the one you don't."

She shook her head before he finished. "I didn't even know you were the devil until that day." She shut her eyes and rubbed her temples. "We could have made that decision together, but you took it out of my hands."

"It's not like I went to work and decided I was going to implode my life."

Tilly walked out with two large glasses of iced tea. "You'll need this. It's extra cold and super sweet if anger and bitterness take over your conversation." She turned to leave but stopped and spun back around. "Welcome back, Miles."

"Thanks, Tilly." He brought the glass to his lips and let the sweetness coat the sour and bitterness he felt throughout his body.

They sat silent until Ollie sauntered over, shimmied under the table, and laid on Emmaline's feet.

"Does he always have to be touching me?" She looked down. "And why is he licking my shoe?"

"Is it the left shoe?"

"Yes. Why?"

He shrugged. "He likes what he likes."

"He's a nuisance."

"He's loyal, and that counts for something."

She picked up her cold glass and touched it to her forehead, rolling it back and forth until the condensation dripped from her skin. "Was that a dig at me?"

"I didn't intend it to be, but I can see how it sounds now that it's out."

"Look, what happened was a tragedy, but it was probably for the best."

That was his thought for years, too. "Was it? Look at us. You're married to the resort, and I..."

"Got a hairy boyfriend who drools. Does he sleep with you?"

He laughed. "Yes, but I don't share my pillow."

Tilly showed back up with a charcuterie board and silverware. "Sorry to interrupt, but Em's only eaten a quart of ice cream, a pie, and a sticky bun. She needs proper food." She set it in front of them and pretended to tiptoe away. "I didn't give you knives. I figured it was safer that way," she yelled when she reached the kitchen door.

"A quart of ice cream? Because of me?"

She waved her hand in the air. "Don't be ridiculous. I got over you thirty years ago. Even then, I didn't eat a bucket of French vanilla and a pecan pie."

"A whole pie?"

"I had a lot of processing to do." She unrolled her cloth napkin and pulled out a fork to stab a piece of salami and a slice of cheese. "Did you know a travel critic is coming to town? I'm certain they'll stay at The Brown."

"Is that why I've got a to-do list you'd only give a bitter enemy?" He pulled it out of his pocket. "Rake the sand? Deadhead the flowers? What does that even mean?"

"You have to pinch the dead bits off to stimulate growth."

"I didn't know that. How do flowers survive in the wild?"

She hesitated, then blinked rapidly. "I never thought of that. It doesn't matter because they look better when they're well-groomed."

"And you don't have a gardener for that?"

With hunched shoulders, she slumped forward. "Okay, I was mad at you for showing up when I made the list." She smiled. "This is the second one. The first one the girls made me throw away."

"What was on it?"

She breathed deeply and let the breath swoosh from her lungs. "De-barnacle the pier?"

"You must have been irate."

"Yes, I was, but now I'm hungry, and my mind is on something else, which is a good thing for you because I was so angry. Angry enough that I could do bodily injury."

"Then Tilly is smart to omit the knives."

She picked up her fork and looked at it. "Not sharp enough to matter." She let out a peal of laughter, then covered her mouth. "Sorry. I don't know what came over me."

"To clear things up once and for all. I didn't expect things to go the way they did. It happened so fast. I caught my father doctoring the details on a sales receipt and called him on it. I didn't see that others were in the room. That information got passed around like a bottle of Crown on prom night. There was no taking it back, but you must understand that I confronted my father because he was cheating the system. The same system your father was getting ready to invest a sizeable amount of cash in. I didn't go to work that day thinking I'd sabotage my life. Who does that?"

"But you destroyed both of our lives."

He reached for an olive and popped it into his mouth. "I thought your dad would be proud of me for saving him the embarrassment of going into business with my father."

"You did save him."

"But he used it against me. Not only did he refuse to let

me marry you, but he convinced you I wasn't worthy." He cleared his throat. "All that time, I thought you had fallen in love with me, but that was only half the story. You were attracted to the prestige of my family."

She laughed so hard she snorted. "Oh, please. I'm a Brown. I don't need anyone else's influence."

"Once you married me, you would have lost that name, and you'd be a despicable McClintock."

She lowered her head. "What was I to do? I was twenty, and my father laid it out in plain and simple terms. If I'd left with you, I'd never have been allowed back. He would not let me ruin everything he'd built. He stood under that willow tree and told me I'd be cut off."

His heart sank into the pit of his empty stomach to comingle with the single olive he ate. He knew it was all about money. "It's always about the money with the Browns, isn't it?"

Her head snapped back like he'd slapped her in the face. "What are you talking about?"

"You chose money over love."

She threaded her fingers into her hair and pulled at her roots. "I chose to survive. I chose my family. You forsook yours."

"No, I was honorable, and they disowned me. You … you chose the easy way out. You chose air conditioning and five-star meals. High thread counts and Tempur-Pedic mattresses. I was supposed to be your family, but you didn't pick me." He pointed to the various points of the resort. "I hope it makes you happy because if you keep choosing the resort, that's all you'll get."

"It's enough."

"You were many things when we were younger, like funny and sexy and rebellious, but you were never a liar."

She growled, and poor Ollie shot from under the table to take cover by his side. "Why is everyone calling me a liar?"

He lifted a shoulder. "If it looks like a duck and walks like a duck, it's probably a duck." He pulled his legs from under the table and stood. "I sure miss my Emmaline. If she ever resurfaces, let me know."

"Where are you going?" She slammed her hands on the table, causing several items to rise and roll off. Ollie was happy to help with the clean-up by gobbling the runaway cheese and tomato.

"I've got a lot of work to do." He picked up his list.

"But we're not finished talking."

Everything about him wanted to sit back down, but what good would it do? Until Emmaline realized there was more to life than The Brown Resort, she had no place in his.

"I'm finished listening." He took another look at the list. "I should complete this by tomorrow. You can leave your next list with Margot."

"What about tomorrow? We can meet for dinner and talk about things."

"Sorry, I've already got a date."

CHAPTER SEVEN

D id she hear him correctly? She shook her head and then processed his words again.

Tilly arrived with a bottle of wine and two glasses. "That didn't turn out the way I expected." She pulled a corkscrew from her pocket and opened the bottle of cabernet. The sun was setting and cast an orange glow on the nearby sand. It was a date-worthy scene, and she spent it with Tilly, who filled the wineglass half-full.

"He said he had a date."

Tilly tipped the bottle and filled it to the rim. "I know."

"You knew he had a date and still brought us a date-worthy appetizer?" She took in the beautiful display of meats, cheeses, jams, and a real honeycomb. This whole setup was proposal-worthy. Not that she was looking for anything like that.

Tilly pulled off her chef's jacket and rolled it into a ball before taking a seat. "I was feeding my friend. And while I might have had hopes for a reconciliation, I would have settled for a truce."

Em sipped her wine and set her glass down before she

picked up a cracker and loaded it with artisanal cheese and honeycomb.

"Oh, we have an understanding. He hates me, and I hate me." She took a bite. "How do you know he has a date?"

Tilly sighed. "I saw the reservation back inside when I checked the numbers for tomorrow."

Em's mouth hung open. "He's bringing her to The Brown to eat?" She picked up a chunk of cheese and a piece of prosciutto and shoved them into her mouth. As she chewed, she simmered inside. "He's punishing me."

Tilly laughed. "Sounds like you're punishing each other."

Em frowned. "My punishment doesn't hurt his heart. Whereas he kills me with a thousand tiny cuts." She gulped her wine and filled it back up. "Do you have grease traps or something awful that needs to be cleaned in the kitchen? I can add it to tomorrow's list."

Tilly picked up a piece of salami. "You know what I like about salty meat? You can't have just one piece. I've tried, but you get a little taste of something that delicious, and you just need more."

Em stared at her friend in disbelief. "I'm having a life crisis, and all you can talk about is salami?"

Tilly grinned. "I'm giving you a solution, silly."

"What do you mean?"

Tilly rolled up the piece of salami and stuck it in her mouth. She moaned and hummed and closed her eyes like she was in ecstasy. When she opened them again, she said, "Mmm, one piece is never enough." She picked up another slice and tossed it at Em. "It's time you took a lesson from the salami, but you'll need the girls' help. I can tell you to look delicious, but my skills remain in the culinary arts. I'm no miracle worker with beauty. You'll need Charlotte for that." She picked up her glass of wine and left Em alone on the picnic bench.

She picked up her phone and took a selfie because she couldn't figure out what everyone was talking about, but all day long, people had been commenting on her looks, and not in a flattering way.

When she glanced at the photo, she gasped. She couldn't believe she let herself out of the house looking like she was. If her mama were alive, she'd be madder than a wet hen because Em looked like one with her makeup gone and her lipstick talked off. Her hair looked like she'd passed through a car wash with her head out the window.

Tilly didn't have to worry about her being like a bite of salami, all tempting and delicious. She looked like the meat —ground up and aged, before it was shoved into a sleeve and sliced into delicious perfection. No wonder Miles had a date. It was probably with someone cute, sweet, and appetizing.

She sat alone and sipped her wine while devouring the entire tray herself. She might as well make it a complete disaster. By tomorrow, she'd have to shove this year's butt in last year's jeans. It would be like putting ten pounds of taters in a five-pound sack, but what did she care? No one was looking at her taters, anyway. As she swirled the last piece of baguette into the honey, she considered Tilly's advice. Did she want to be something Miles craved?

Her eternal teenager screamed yes, but the woman she'd become wasn't so sure. She'd been fine all these years without him. She didn't need Miles to make her feel beautiful. She had Charlotte for that. As she pulled out her phone to text her friend, she told herself it had nothing to do with Miles and everything to do with the travel critic, who would undoubtedly show up. There was no way she'd be caught looking less than perfect.

She typed a message to Charlotte.

I need a makeover. Can you help?

Charlotte responded immediately.

Oh, honey. That's what I do. Is this about Miles's date?

Were there no secrets in town?

Did Tilly tell you? She watched the dots dance across her screen and disappear several times before the reply popped up.

I cannot divulge my source.

She knew her source. She could deny this had anything to do with Miles, but her friends knew her too well. Even so, she liked having deniability.

This isn't about Miles. He's already in my rearview mirror. This is about representing The Brown, and I can't do that if I look like something that washed up on shore during the last storm.

There were more dots and pauses before Charlotte replied. *I'll be there at eight.*

She was about to complain about the early hour, but another message came in.

Before you whine about the time, look at what I have to work with and be grateful I didn't say seven. Have the coffee ready.

If she were getting Charlotte's full treatment, she wouldn't have time to train Miles on anything tomorrow, and she didn't have the heart to give him another list of items. She marched herself into the empty lobby of The Kessler.

"Margot?"

Up she popped from behind the desk with a mouthful of food.

"Em." She swallowed and wiped her mouth with the back of her hand. "Sorry, I didn't have time to eat."

All staff members got one thirty-minute and two ten-minute breaks each day. "Did you take your break?"

Margot looked everywhere but at Em. "I did."

"Why didn't you eat? What did you do on your break?"

Margot wasn't the girl who blushed, but her cheeks turned choke cherry red. "I ... I ..." She shook her head. "What I do on my time is my business."

Em couldn't argue with her. "But what you do on my time is my business and eating on the job is unprofessional." She knew Margot and knew exactly what she was doing with her own time. If she still saw the chef from The Brown, she knew who she was doing on her lunch break. "Tomorrow, you'll be training Miles on the front counter." She peeked over the desk at the plate of fries and the half-eaten burger on the shelf. "Set a good example."

"I'm always good." She giggled. "At least that's what they say."

"I bet your mama's proud," Em said.

Margot smiled. "She is. This job is something she can tell people about." Margot rounded the desk and wrapped Em in a hug. "I'm grateful you saw something in me and took a chance. I know you had your doubts, but I'll make you proud, too." She stepped back, and Margot looked like a kid seeking approval for a second. Em knew what that felt like. She was always looking for her parents' endorsement but never got it. All their praise was lavished on her sister Olivia, who was their first choice to take over The Brown. When her parents passed, Em inherited half of the property but was told it would be better if she were a silent partner. Maybe that was part of her drive to make the resort successful. No one expected her to succeed, and yet, she had. She hadn't bankrupted it or burned it down in the years since she'd been in charge.

Em felt terrible for the thoughts she had about Margot. Not everyone was cut from the same cloth, and poor Margot was burlap in a room of Egyptian cotton. Maybe Margot needed someone to believe in her so she could believe in herself.

"Make sure to show Miles everything I taught you about guest etiquette."

Margot laughed. "Don't worry. I'll show him everything I know."

That was what she was afraid of, but everyone deserved a chance to shine.

She walked out and rounded the building to the private residence where Miles was staying. She pulled back her shoulders and raised her hand to knock. Just before her knuckles connected with the door, it opened, and Miles was there wearing a pair of swim trunks and nothing else.

"Hello, Emmaline." He stopped and looked at her. "Did you need me?"

She shook her head so hard that she scrambled her brains. "No. I don't need you."

"Yes. That's right. You keep reminding me." He stepped onto the porch to make room for Ollie to join him. As soon as the dog came out, he went immediately for her left shoe and licked it.

"He has a serious problem."

Miles smiled, and her heart picked up its pace. "He's in a twelve-step program but stuck at the first step because he won't admit he has a problem."

She tried to keep a straight face, but a giggle escaped, leading to a full laugh. Miles always made her laugh.

"It's nice to see you haven't lost your ability to enjoy a moment, Emmaline."

She got herself under control, which was hard, given that she was standing there staring at his bare chest and wondering if the hair there was as coarse as it looked or was it soft to the touch. Way back when they were together, he only had a few hairs. She had to pull a stray hair or two from places they didn't belong on her, so maybe his chest hair was simply a sign of age and maturity. Oh, who was she kidding? That hair was pure male virility. It took everything in her to drag her eyes from his body and lift them to look at his face.

"Did you need something?" He pulled his phone from his pocket. "I thought I was off after I finished your list, but if you need me to do something else…"

"No. You're fine." He was fine. Damn fine, but that wasn't the point. "I'm here to let you know that you'll be working with Margot tomorrow."

His eyes widened. "You must really hate me."

She took a deep breath. "Of course … not. I'm just doing my job to ensure you're trained to do yours."

"No to-do list?"

"No. Where are you off to?"

He nodded toward the water. "I heard the dock needs barnacle removal."

"I took that off the list."

He winked. "Only because your friends made you."

She shrugged. "True, but it's unnecessary."

"And yet, I'd do it if you asked."

"You would?"

He nodded. "There isn't much I wouldn't do for you, Emmaline."

"Except stay all those years ago."

He walked past her. "I would have stayed if you'd

asked. If you had decided you wanted me in your life." He tapped his leg, and Ollie followed him down the walk toward The Kessler dock.

He had a point. Those who don't ask never get. She supposed the worst answer would have been no had she asked him to stay. Maybe that's why she didn't ask. It was easier to accept Miles's betrayal rather than his rejection. The betrayal was his fault, but the rejection meant something was lacking in her. Hadn't that always been the case?

She returned to her empty charcuterie board and a half-full glass of wine and stared at the sun as it sank into the ocean.

"Nice view," Tilly said from behind.

Miles set his phone on the dock's rail and pet Ollie before diving into the water. "It sure is."

CHAPTER EIGHT

Miles walked out his door at five minutes to eight for his shift at the front desk. He half-expected to find a honey-do list taped to his door. Carter had warned him there might be one, but nothing was there. He glanced toward The Brown Resort, hoping to glimpse Emmaline, but she was nowhere in sight either. The only sign of life from The Brown staff, and it was questionable whether there was life, was an older man shoveling ashes from the beach's fire pit to a wheelbarrow. He strained to see the man because he looked familiar. Could that be Hugh? If so, he had to be a hundred years old.

He had three minutes until his shift started, and he debated whether to go inside or confirm his suspicions. Curiosity got the better of him.

"Let's go, Ollie." He tapped his leg and half-jogged to where the man struggled to lift the shovel. When he got there, he reached for it. "Let me help you."

The older man turned to face him. "Eh?" he yelled and pointed to his ear. "Can't hear ya."

With ears that size, he should have been able to hear

him from across the lake. Miles took the shovel and stepped closer. "Let me help you," he said, loud enough for Cricket in the diner to hear. "Hugh, right?"

"Miles?" The old geezer tilted his head left and right and smiled. "Is that you?"

"Yes, sir." In a few scoops, he had the ashes in the wheelbarrow. "Where does this go?"

Hugh pointed to the house behind the resort. "There's a dumpster over yonder."

"I got it." He placed the shovel on top of the cooled ashes and spent logs and lifted the handles. He hated being late to work, but Hugh was too old to do this kind of work. "Isn't there anyone else to help you?"

Hugh shook his head. "I'm the ash man." He gave him a sly smile. "Seventy years ago, I could have dropped the h and added an s." He chuckled. "The mind is still willing, but the body gave up long ago."

His hearing might have faded, but his sense of humor remained. "Why are you working? You've got to be eighty." He was being conservative with his guess.

"I'm ninety-two, and I work because my Mabel tells me she'd murder me if I stayed home. Besides, she's got an expensive QVC habit that needs my paycheck to support. There's not a lot I can give her, but I can provide her with Today's Special Value money."

"They say, happy wife, happy life. I'm sure Mabel is an amazing woman and incredibly happy."

Hugh grinned. "I keep telling her that, and she makes me spaghetti and meatballs."

Miles wheeled close to the dumpster and evaluated the situation. Once the wheelbarrow was full, Hugh had to bring it to the dumpster and then transfer it by shovel. That was a lot of shoveling for an older man, and from the wheelbarrow to the dumpster, he had to lift the shovel nearly to his shoulders. As a strong man, even he dumped a few ashes sideways.

"Not an ideal setup here."

Hugh shook his head. "Nope, but this is how it's been done since I can remember. No sense changing something that doesn't need it."

Ollie sidled over to Hugh and looked longingly at his left boot. "Not today, Ollie."

Hugh pointed to the dog. "Has Em seen him? There are no dogs allowed at the resort."

Miles sighed. "You're right. I should get him back to The Kessler, where fur friends are appreciated."

"The Kessler?"

Miles leaned the wheelbarrow and shovel against the house before turning toward The Kessler. He was already ten minutes late. "I'm managing the property for Carter and Brie while they're on their honeymoon."

Hugh's bushy white brows rose an inch on his lined forehead. "And Em knows this?"

"She does."

"And she's okay with it."

"Nope, but we don't always get what we want."

"You remember Em, right? She's a woman who always gets what she wants."

Miles considered Emmaline for a few seconds. "She's trained you to believe that. But I don't know if she understands what she truly wants. I think Emmaline has been told what she wants, and she doesn't know any different."

Hugh, Ollie, and Miles walked back toward the front of the resort.

"You might be on to something there. I'm trained to want what Mabel wants."

"Which is fine if you want the same thing." The problem for Miles was he wasn't sure what he wanted. He thought it was Emmaline, but there would be no room for him as long as her number one priority was the resort. She'd chosen it over him years ago, and he refused to come in second in her life again. "Have a good morning, Hugh. Don't work yourself to death. If you need help with something, just come and ask." He nodded behind him to The Kessler. "I'll be right there."

He and Ollie left Hugh standing on the sidewalk. To wait for him would make him another fifteen minutes late, and he didn't want to set a poor example. Though Margot was training him, he was, for all intents and purposes, the manager there.

As he passed the parking lot, he saw Charlotte and Marybeth exit a car. They both stopped and stared.

"Good morning, ladies." He nodded and walked up the steps and into The Kessler.

"You're late," Margot said as she glared at him. "You're not setting the best example, and I'll have to let Em know because she's paying my salary and asked me to keep a close eye on you."

"What will it cost me to keep that bit of information secret?"

Margot tapped her chin and smiled. "I'll leave it out of my daily report for twenty bucks."

He whipped his wallet out of his back pocket and took out a twenty. Margot needed to value herself more. He would have given her a hundred. "Done."

"And an extra fifteen minutes on my lunch break. It's hard to get it all in in thirty."

He didn't know what she was getting in, but he knew

many women like Margot, and he could guess. "Deal. Now, where do we start?"

She winked and puckered her lips. "The bedroom, of course." She swiped up a ring of keys. "We had a few early checkouts, and we need to ensure they vacated before cleaning the rooms. Follow me."

She led him down the hallway and stopped in front of a room called the Aloha Suite.

"There are suites here?"

She shrugged and laughed. "It ain't the Ritz, but it's better than Motel 6."

He imagined she'd only been to one of those, so he didn't know what she was using for a reference, but he went with it.

She knocked and waited and then opened the door with her master key. Ollie walked patiently by Miles's side, being the good boy that he was.

"I check the rooms first because if there's something left behind, I want first dibs if it doesn't get claimed because this is the most expensive room in the place, and they probably have the best stuff. I don't see them calling me for their lost shit." She walked through the empty room and opened drawers before tossing the sheets back. "Just last week, someone left a La Perla teddy. I've got twenty pounds to lose before I fit into it, but it gives me something to look forward to."

"You want some woman's used lingerie?" He couldn't imagine. Then again, he didn't know what La Perla was. He knew the word teddy because, in his memory, Emmaline had some sexy ones. She had a red lace number that always made him grateful she was his.

"Once it's washed, it's like new, and since I found it between the sheets, it's got to be get-lucky lace, right?"

"You and I should talk about setting your standards a little higher."

Her eyes got buggy and scary looking. "Higher than La Perla? Are you nuts? I looked that scrap of material up, and it cost four hundred and ninety dollars."

He had to give Margot credit. She knew her lingerie. If he'd found it, he would have tossed it in the bucket without a second thought.

She opened the closet and sighed. "Not a thing left behind."

"Maybe next time."

"Probably not. I googled the guest checking in today, and she looks like a grandma."

"What's wrong with grandmas?"

She rolled her eyes twice before she stared at him. "Flannel pajamas and fuzzy slippers. Who wants that?"

Once again, she made a valid point. His mother had worn nothing but flannel pj's and those fuzzy socks with the rubber soles, so she didn't slip.

"How many things do you have dibs on in those boxes?"

She looked at the ceiling and counted her fingers. She went through her digits at least three times.

"Thirty-three if you count the white cotton bun huggers left by Clint Eastwood."

"Clint Eastwood was here? I thought The Kessler has only been open for a few weeks."

She lifted her shoulders and let them fall heavily with a sigh. "Okay, it probably wasn't him because he stayed in a regular room, but the man looked like him, and I snuck his photo." She pulled her phone from her back pocket and scrolled through her pics. "See?" She pointed to a speck on the photo. From a distance, he could pass for Clint.

"I could sell his tighty whiteys on eBay for a pretty penny."

"You can't steal underwear and sell them on eBay."

"Oh, I forgot you were the boss." She let out a not-so-feminine growl. "Now I need to figure out a new side gig."

Lord help them. "How about you focus on your job, and we look into incentives?" He thought of a dozen ways that would work for Margot. All she had to do was stop touching the guests, and he'd give her a bonus.

"Really?" She narrowed her eyes. "What would I have to do?" She placed her fists on her hips. "I have standards, you know."

He wanted to roll his eyes. If Margot had standards, they were pretty low. "How about we start with something easy, like no hugging the guests unless you've known them personally for five years or more?"

She shook her head and frowned. "I knew you weren't going to be any fun."

He wanted to tell her he was plenty of fun, but he didn't want anything he said to be misconstrued as an invitation.

They left the room, locked it, and headed to the next room and the next until they'd visited five vacant properties.

"When does housekeeping come?"

She laughed. "Here's the thing. We're short-staffed today, so you and I get to clean rooms."

"Really? Are you often short-staffed?"

"Nope. This is the first time."

This had Emmaline written all over it.

CHAPTER NINE

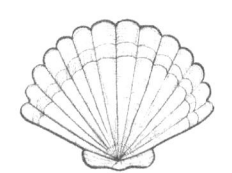

Em answered the knock at the door to find two of her best friends standing there, all flushed. Charlotte hadn't been that pink in the cheeks since Ryder Watkins asked her to prom over thirty years ago.

"What is going on? You two look like you saw the Chippendales revue and ran out of ones."

Charlotte snorted. "Honey, when's the last time you went to a male revue?"

She thought about it and pointed to Marybeth. "I've never been, but we hired that stripper for Tilly's birthday that time."

Charlotte walked past her, pulling a small suitcase. "They prefer fives these days with inflation and all. That oil they slick themselves with that smells so yummy must be expensive."

Em waited for Marybeth to come inside. "It's probably olive oil."

She moved into the kitchen and waved the girls forward. "I made coffee."

Marybeth's nose scrunched. "I feared as much and

asked Tilly to bring us a pot of the good stuff and a few of those cinnamon buns I know she made this morning." She cleared her throat. "Umm, speaking of buns, I see you've got Miles working his off."

She wanted to snicker, but her mama taught her better. "He's doing exactly what he came to The Kessler to do ... run it." She smiled. "It's a real shame his staff called in sick today."

Charlotte pushed her suitcase to the side and flopped into one chair that circled the small round table. Em loved the table with its ceramic base covered in vines and flowers that led to the glass top. It was a secret garden growing in her kitchen. One that didn't need fertilizer or water unless she counted the damp paper towels she used to wipe off the dust.

Marybeth looked at the ceiling and said, "Please, God, don't judge her harshly. She may know what she's doing but can't help herself."

"Can you believe that man? He had the audacity to sit at a picnic table last night as if we were friends. And then he told me he had a date, and Tilly confirmed it."

"Did I hear my name?" Tilly called from the front door. "I'm not owning up to anything unless I'm here to defend myself." She entered the kitchen with a pot of coffee and a tray of sweets, which included three world-famous cinnamon rolls, several cookies, and a chunk of walnut fudge. "It's a little early for all this, but desperate times and all."

"I told the girls that Miles had a date, and you confirmed it."

Tilly set her bounty on the table and walked to the cupboard to get four mugs. "That's why you girls are here."

She pointed to Em. "We all know she's lovely, but lately, she's—"

Em waved her hand in front of her face. "Let's face it. I look like something you drag in on the bottom of your shoe." She rubbed her eyes.

"Don't do that," Charlotte said. "You'll give yourself more wrinkles."

Em took a seat next to Charlotte. "Girl, have you seen my eyes? My wrinkles are multiplying like flies on a dead fish. I honey a few off; a week later, I've got six more."

Charlotte thumbed at the bottom of her eyes. "Have you been using that cream I gave you?" Em must have delayed a few seconds too long because Charlotte huffed. "Leave that honey alone. It's too heavy, and honestly, it does nothing for no one."

Em broke off a chunk of fudge and brought it to her lips. "That's not true. Ollie liked it plenty. He licked it off my face." She cocked her head and smiled. "I think he took a few crow's feet with him. Maybe that's the ticket. I can slather my face with Cricket's honey and then get Miles's silly dog to clean me up." She popped the fudge into her mouth and hummed. Tilly made the best fudge. Oh, who was she kidding? Tilly made the best of everything. After she swallowed, she said, "Cheaper than a facelift."

Tilly took the last unoccupied seat. "People say that dogs have clean mouths but just remember they were probably licking their butts seconds before your face."

Charlotte made a gagging sound. "Yuck. Use my cream. It's more effective." She scrunched her nose. "And hygienic." She rose and went to the small suitcase, laid it on its side, and opened it. Inside were dozens of vials and tubes and brushes.

"Are you moving in?" Em asked.

Charlotte pulled a scrunchy from the bag and tossed it at Em. "Big jobs require big tools. Now put your hair up."

"I get that, but do you think I'll need all that?" She eyed the bag again and couldn't imagine needing a tenth of what was in it.

Charlotte looked at her and then back at the bag. "I probably should have brought both bags, but we'll make do." She tapped her chin. "Tell me, are we enhancing what we've got, or are we going all out and turning back the clock thirty years?"

Em's jaw dropped open. She wasn't sure which caused the reaction—that she'd need two suitcases to make her presentable, or that there was a possibility of turning back the clock thirty years without a scalpel. "You can do that?"

Charlotte took out a tube and a small brush. "No, but a girl can dream. Are you trying to make him jealous?" She set her supplies on the table and went to the sink, where she wet a few paper towels, returned, and accosted Em's face like a mother did after her kid ate cotton candy. The blue kind that dyed everything within an inch of the mouth and took a week to fade.

"Give me that. If you keep scrubbing at me like a dirty barbecue grill, I won't have a face left." She gently removed any makeup remnants.

"We'll start with a gentle peel, making your skin as smooth as a baby's bottom."

"If that's the stuff you put on Brie, I'll pass. She said it felt like hellfire."

Charlotte ignored her and spread a glop of goo on her face. At first, it was cold, but something happened after it sat there for a few seconds. She rethought her barbecue statement because the goop was like hot coals, and her face was screaming for an extinguisher.

Em reached for the stack of napkins on the table, but Charlotte stopped her with a screech. "Don't you dare. I just put twenty dollars' worth on your face."

"And I'll need ten grand in reconstructive surgery when you're finished."

Tilly shrugged. "It's not the ideal way to get a facelift, but..."

Rather than face Charlotte's wrath, she took the napkins and fanned herself. She turned to Marybeth. "You should start praying this eases up in a few minutes, or I'm going to strangle our friend and the quartet becomes a trio."

Marybeth slapped her hands together like she was going to pray but said, "Don't you dare murder her before my fundraiser. She's doing my makeup for that event."

The pain subsided, and Em dropped the napkins but picked up another bite of fudge. Before she could get it in her mouth, Charlotte plucked it from her lips. "Sugar is the devil when it comes to aging. Do you want to look like Agnes Willoughby? She's fifty and looks eighty."

Marybeth had a cookie in her hand and dropped it. "I thought she was eighty."

Em picked up the cookie and handed it back to Marybeth. "She is eighty. She's friends with my granny, so she's getting there in age." She pointed to Charlotte. "Stop trying to scare us."

"Stop threatening murder." She pointed to the sink. "Go rinse."

Em did, and she had to admit that her face felt like a baby's bottom. Not that she'd touched many, but she knew they were soft like brand new skin. As soon as she took a seat, Charlotte slathered on something else that was cool and heavenly. She spent the next twenty minutes applying and removing creams and gels.

Once Em was sufficiently moisturized, Charlotte sat beside her and laid out an extensive palette of colors and several brushes. "What's our aim? Do you want him back? Or do you want him to regret he ever left you?"

"Want him back? Heavens, no. I had no idea how overweight I was back then, but Miles leaving town was like getting a Lap Band and losing a hundred and eighty pounds of excess."

"Okay, then we'll make him regret ever leaving, and when he wants you back, all you have to do is Nancy Reagan him," Charlotte said.

"What does that mean?" Em reached out, grabbed the last piece of fudge, and ate it before anyone could say a word.

Tilly raised her hand. "Even I know that." She sipped her coffee. "Just say no."

It was an eighties reference to drugs. The problem was, in her memory, Miles was the best kind of drug. He was the one who had her screaming *yes, yes, yes* in the boathouse at ungodly hours of the night.

"I have no interest in Miles." She gave Tilly a look she hoped would silence her. Only Tilly was close enough daily to see how his presence affected her. "I don't care if he has a date." Her throat closed on the last word because it was a bitter lie. "I hate the man." That left her lips smoothly because it was mostly the truth. She hated him because he made her feel the same way he did then—breathless. Then again, maybe she was coming down with something. Could a person catch asthma? Probably not, so it was reasonable to blame Miles.

"Then why am I wasting my good stuff if you don't care?"

Em sat up taller. "Investing in your friends is never a

waste. Besides, don't forget the travel critic could be here, and we don't want her seeing me and writing something about the old crone who runs The Brown." She picked up a nearby mirror. "I'll tell everyone who will listen that you do my makeup."

Charlotte gasped and rose from her seat. She studied Em the way an artist scrutinizes a canvas. "We'd better get to work. I'm no Picasso, and you're no Mona Lisa."

"It's a good thing because da Vinci painted the Mona Lisa. Picasso painted his lover, and I swear she had two noses and several eyes," Em said.

While Charlotte worked on her makeup, Marybeth went upstairs to rummage through her closet. At the mention of a fashion show, Tilly rushed for the door, claiming that she expected a major lunch rush.

When Charlotte finished, she wouldn't let Em see the final results. She said it was better to look at the finished product as a whole. A cake wasn't as lovely without the frosting. Em tried to make the case that Charlotte's contribution was the cake and the frosting, but she didn't win.

In her room, Marybeth displayed two outfits and a frown. "You and I are going shopping. There isn't one label I recognize except Levi." She shook the hanger in her right hand which held a pair of jeans, a white eyelet shirt and a pink cardigan. It was sweet and reminded her of her more youthful days. She knew precisely what Marybeth was going for. In her other hand was a little black dress. It was so tiny that if she bent over, she would become an underwear model.

"I'll take the jeans."

Marybeth smiled. "Wise choice. You don't want to put everything you got on the showroom floor. Save a little magic for the test drive."

"I've test-driven him before. Don't forget that man put his truck in gear and raced from town."

Marybeth clucked. "Have you forgotten that your daddy was pointing a shotgun at him?"

"Was he?"

She stared at Marybeth and then at Charlotte.

"We're talking about your father. If he wanted Miles gone, he'd see to it that he left," Charlotte said.

"Your father may have had the gun, but you're the one who shot the bullet straight through that boy's heart."

Why did she keep forgetting that she told him to leave? *Because it was so much easier to blame someone else when she made a mistake.*

She dressed and was allowed to look in the mirror. She wasn't wearing fancy clothes, but when she put on her pageant smile, she was pleased.

"If he wants you back, what will you do?"

She stared at the woman in the mirror who reminded her of the girl she used to be. Once again, her heart said yes, but her mind said she didn't need a man to define her.

"I honestly don't know." And that was the truth. She was at war with herself. When it came to a battle within, there were no winners.

CHAPTER TEN

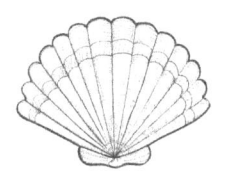

As he walked into Carter and Brie's place, Miles wondered how people did that work daily. He'd had a lot of hard jobs in his life. Ranching was the most exhausting thing he'd ever done until he'd worked a full day at the Kessler cleaning rooms and taking care of their guests' needs. He'd hauled luggage, delivered meals from The Brown's kitchen because apparently, they were short-staffed too, and cleaned all ten rooms with the help of Margot, who wasn't much help because she was told to supervise him. He was grateful they'd only opened the resort's first floor because he didn't have it in him to clean another ten rooms.

If he hadn't invited his mother and Cormac to The Brown for dinner, he would have microwaved a frozen burrito and called it a night. Everything on him, from his toes to his hair, hurt. How did hair hurt? Then he remembered looking under the beds for left-behind items and whacking his noggin on the bedside table on his way up.

He took off his shirt and tossed it on a nearby chair before heading down the hallway. He made a beeline for the refrigerator, took one of Carter's beers, twisted the cap off, and drank half of it down.

Ollie stood next to him, wagging his tail. He looked a little worn, too, given that his daily naps had to occur in several locations.

"Hey, buddy." He reached into the pocket of his jeans and pulled out one of the treats he always had on him. "You earned this." Ollie found the only left-behind item today. It was a shoe. Not a left shoe, but a right one, so he brought it to Miles and dropped it at his feet. Had it been a left, Miles would have had to fight him for it, and to be honest, he probably would have let Ollie keep it because he didn't have the energy for a game of tug-of-war.

With about forty minutes to relax before his mother and Cormac showed up, he flopped onto the sofa and leaned back on the cushions. He'd been there for only a minute when someone knocked at the door.

If it was Margot wanting to rub his back again, he would have a fit. They'd talked at length about appropriate behavior, but she had her own set of rules.

He tried two times to get off the sofa before he dragged himself to the door. The last person he expected to find was Emmaline when he opened it. She stood there looking pretty in a pink sweater, a white blouse, and jeans that fit her like a glove. On her feet were bejeweled sandals that showed her pretty painted toes.

"Emmaline." His voice cracked like a pubescent teen. His body responded because she looked exactly like she had decades ago. Everything on the outside was spun sugar, but her eyes danced with mischief, and he remembered what being around her then felt like. It was heavenly.

She stared at his bare chest for what seemed like an eternity. All that looking made his jeans tighter, and when her eyes dropped, they were both aware of what her presence did to him.

He moved forward so they were inches apart. "Did you need something?" Ollie bound around the corner and took a running jump, catching her on the hip and sending her tottering backward. Miles grabbed for her and pulled her into his arms.

"Ollie!" His stern voice sent the dog running for cover. He dashed back inside and ran down the hallway toward the bedroom. Miles knew if he followed, he'd find Ollie's head under the bed and his hind end exposed. For an intelligent dog, he didn't understand hiding.

Emmaline in his arms brought him back to a time when he thought his life was perfect. She felt the same, smelled the same, and her curves fit him just right.

"Your dog is a nuisance." She could have stepped back, but she didn't. Instead, she leaned into him and inhaled.

"Are you smelling me?" He caught her in the act. Emmaline always loved his cologne. He hadn't changed it in all these years. If something was working, why fix it?

She jumped back. "Are you crazy?"

"No. I'm observant, and if I remember correctly, you always liked my cologne."

She leaned in and sniffed. "You need a shower if you have a date. You smell like a construction worker who hasn't bathed in days."

He lifted his arm and sniffed. "My deodorant is working."

"If you say so." She looked past him to the beer on the table. "Rough day?"

He'd never confess to being dog-tired and ass-dragging by dinnertime. "It was a good day." He stepped aside. "You want a beer?"

There was a great debate going on in her brain. He could see it by the way her head cocked side to side.

"I could use a beer."

Miles moved to the kitchen, grabbed another beer for her, popped the cap, and handed it over. He would have offered her a glass, but Emmaline never used one. She always said pouring it into another container reduced the fizz. "Was it a busy day for you too?"

She took a sip. "It was no different from the others." She smiled and leaned against the kitchen counter.

The old kitchen was dated, and Emmaline looked out of place. It was like putting a peanut butter and jelly sandwich on fine china and serving it with a glass of milk in a crystal goblet.

"Really? I was told you were short-handed," he said.

"Oh. That. We handled it. What about you? You were shorthanded too, I heard."

He shrugged. "Yes, but we also handled it as well." He was exhausted, but wouldn't let her see that. It only showed weakness and gave her the upper hand.

"Good to know." She pushed away from the counter and walked into the living room. "This place needs to be gutted like a fish."

He took in the space. Gutting it might have been extreme, but it needed work. "I'll be painting while I'm here." Whether they sold the resort or stayed, it needed a pick-me-up, and a coat of paint would do wonders.

"You paint?"

He laughed. "Not really, but how hard can it be?"

"Pretty damn hard if you want it to look good."

He made a face and shrugged. "They said nothing about it looking nice."

Her beautiful eyes widened. "You're not doing a half-assed job. My niece and nephew have to live here."

He moved close to her, so her sweater-covered breasts touched his bare chest. "Now, darlin', have you ever known me to do anything halfway?" He leaned in until his lips brushed the lobe of her ear. "I'm always thorough." He swore she shivered before she stepped back.

"Last time we were together, you thoroughly ruined everything."

Would she ever let it go? He knew she wouldn't until he proved himself trustworthy. When he left, everyone, including Emmaline, considered him lower than dirt. He needed to change people's opinions of him.

"You're right, and I'm sorry."

"At least we agree on something."

"Don't forget, you could have come with me."

A low growl came from her throat. "Do we have to go over it again?"

He shook his head. "Nope." He picked up his beer and looked at his phone. "You came here for a reason, and I'm sure it wasn't to drink a beer and chitchat about old times."

She brought the beer to her mouth and tipped it back, gulping until it was half finished. "I came to help you get ready for your date. If you want her to think you're a catch, you need to do better than jeans and a T-shirt."

"I'm a grown man, Emmaline. I don't need help to get dressed." As soon as he cast those words out, he wanted to reel them back in. If Emmaline wanted to help dress him, she'd need to help undress him, and he was all about that. "On second thought, you're right. I could use help. This date is incredibly important." He stared into her eyes and watched as the stormy blue churned.

"Oh, how did you meet her?"

He turned and waved her toward the room he was staying in. "One day, I opened my eyes, and she was there." He imagined that was how his once-newborn brain worked.

"Is she pretty?" There was genuine concern in Emmaline's expression.

"She's lovely." His mother was beautiful. Even at seventy-eight and battling cancer, she looked good, but she lived by the eleventh commandment. *Thou shalt not leave home if it took you less than five minutes to get ready.*

They stood in the center of the room, staring at the bed. Emmaline chewed at the bottom of her lip.

"You're not bringing her back here, are you?"

"Are you jealous?" He wasn't sure what he wanted to do about Emmaline and his attraction to her but seeing her here made him want more. How much more was the question.

"Me?" She did that thing where she kicked out a hip, cocked her head, and looked at the ceiling. "Why would I be jealous?"

"Because I think you still love me."

She snorted and rolled her eyes. "I'd rather get pink eye than love you."

"Perfect. Then you'll match your sweater. By the way, you look prettier and sweeter than a ripe peach." He kicked off his boots and unbuttoned his jeans, letting them drop to the carpet. He'd never been a fan of underwear. He'd once heard that confining his junk would overheat his swimmers and make him sterile.

Emmaline tried to keep her eyes on his face, but she couldn't help herself and dropped her gaze. When she licked her lips, he knew she wanted more too.

"I see not much has changed." She stared for a few more seconds. "Lucky girl."

He gripped her shoulders and looked into her eyes. "Would you prefer I don't go on this date? Tell me you love me, Emmaline, and I'll cancel it." He knew she'd never say the words so easily.

"Never. What do I care if you have a date? If it's Margot, you could save yourself a lot of money. She'd be happy to eat at the diner."

"It's not Margot." He moved closer and nuzzled her neck. She didn't push him away or step back. She stretched her neck to the side to give him better access. "Okay, so don't tell me you love me, but admit that you're still interested."

Her hands came between them, and she shoved him back. "I can't believe you're trying to seduce me right before your date." She marched to the door and looked over her shoulder. "Dress yourself." She walked down the hallway.

He smiled when she slammed the door. If she didn't care, she'd never waste her time getting angry. He couldn't wait until she showed up to see his date. He knew she would because Emmaline was curious and couldn't help herself. Hopefully, she wouldn't poison their food.

CHAPTER ELEVEN

She marched into the kitchen and took a seat at the table. It was the perfect vantage point to observe Miles leaving the house and returning with his date. She couldn't wait to see who he brought back.

"What did he say?" Tilly walked from behind the line, pulled off her soiled apron, and sat across from Em. "Did he think you looked beautiful?"

Of course, Tilly had seen her go into Miles's house. She was like a human surveillance system and never missed a thing.

Em thought back to Miles's compliment. "He compared me to fruit."

Tilly stared at her for a moment. "What kind of fruit?"

Em watched The Kessler, hoping to get a glimpse of him leaving. "Does it matter?"

Tilly grunted. "Yes, it matters. Are you a grape or a durian?"

"What the hell is a durian?"

"It's a prickly fruit that smells like sewage."

"And people eat it?"

Tilly shrugged. "Yes. It's the perfect example of why a person shouldn't judge. It's not attractive, but once you get past how it looks and the smell, it tastes like caramel custard topped with whipped cream." She scrunched her nose. "And maybe a little garlic sprinkled on top."

"That sounds awful." She reached for the nearby coffeepot and poured herself a mug. Tilly always had fresh coffee ready. "Apparently, I'm as sweet as a peach."

"That's a good thing." A cook from behind the line called Tilly, and she rose and picked up two plates. When she returned, she set one in front of Em. "Dig in. You'll need a solid meal to survive the night."

Em looked down at a petite filet covered in hollandaise sauce and lumps of crabmeat. Next to it were her favorite scalloped potatoes and grilled asparagus.

"What would I do without you?"

"Eat at Cricket's, and your ass would be the size of an elephant's."

Em chuckled and cut a piece of steak and then swirled it through the rich, creamy sauce. "It's not like you're limiting my calories with this meal."

"I'm providing you with sustainable energy." Tilly took a bite of her steak. "Mmm. What else happened while you were visiting Miles?"

Em dug into the potatoes. "Not much. He invited me in for a beer, and then he got naked."

Tilly choked on her steak. "He what?"

Em closed her eyes and relived the moment. "He was halfway nude when I arrived. No shirt. No shoes. And no inhibitions." She smiled. "It's good to know that some things haven't changed."

"And why did you go there? I thought the big reveal

would be when you showed up at their table looking like dessert."

Em pointed to the window. "You need to stop spying on people."

Tilly raised her brows to make a point. "Says the girl who won't take her eyes off The Kessler for fear of missing something."

She sighed. "Oh, I've been missing something, all right." In a bowl in the center of the table were fruits and veggies, and she picked up the zucchini.

"No way? Was it always like that?"

She'd wiped all memories of Miles from her head because thinking about him made her heart ache, but now that the memory vault was open, she had to admit that nothing below the belt had changed.

After a sigh, she nodded. "Seeing him made me want things I have no business wanting."

"I don't think you ever stopped wanting him. You just told yourself all the reasons you couldn't have him."

"I still can't have him."

Tilly pinched the bridge of her nose. "What's stopping you?"

"Nothing has changed. He's still not a good fit."

Tilly wasn't one to hold back, but the red lifting to her cheeks told Em that she was suppressing a response. After several breaths, Tilly smiled, but it wasn't a genuine smile. It was a smile to cover her disappointment.

"By whose standards? Your father is gone and can't decide for you." She shook her head and made un-lady-like growling sounds. "That mean bastard ruined so many lives."

"Now, Tilly, don't speak of the dead unkindly. He did the best he knew how."

"Yeah, well, so did others like Darth Vader and

Hannibal Lecter. Look at what happened to the people they knew."

"My father didn't boil me in a pot or disembowel me with a light saber."

"No, he eviscerated you and your sister with unkind words. He destroyed your lives by making choices that should have been yours all along. If you don't think he killed you both, you're wrong. You've been the walking dead since Miles left. For the first time in forever, you seem lively."

Em gasped. "Not true. I have a full life. I choose to be single."

Tilly laughed. "Do you?" She took another bite, then another.

"You don't get to be my armchair therapist when you're sitting in the same position."

When Tilly's plate was empty, she sat back and patted her belly. "There's a difference between you and me. I've never had a great love. My lover is food, and I savor him every day."

"And mine is the resort. We are both married. Your spouse is the restaurant, and mine is the rest."

Tilly placed her silverware and napkin on her plate. "How long will you lie to yourself? Don't forget, I've known you forever. I'm the girl who held your hair while you threw up, not because you drank too much but because you were heartsick when he left." She stood. "Also, don't forget that I knew your parents. The resort wasn't passed on to you. You had half a share, but your father didn't want you running it because, I'll say it verbatim: 'You're too spirited, and you'll destroy everything I created. Giving the reins of the resort to you would be like handing matches and kindling to a pyromaniac.'" Tilly huffed. "Those were your father's words, not mine."

"He was wrong. I've run the resort since Olivia died, and nothing has gone wrong."

"True. If he was wrong about that, don't you think he could have been wrong about Miles?"

Tilly stared at Em with a smug expression and then walked away.

Em turned back to the window and saw Miles enter the blind spot at The Brown's entrance. How had she missed him and his date? Damn, Tilly distracted her with thought-provoking comments.

She took a few more bites of everything. Not because she was hungry, but Tilly went to the trouble of ordering her a meal, and she would eat most of it out of respect. When she finished, she cleared her plate and walked to the door.

Tilly called out, "Don't forget what you're missing." She held up a zucchini before she took her butcher knife and chopped it in half.

How could she forget? The image of Miles standing there wearing nothing but a smile would be etched into her brain forever. Knowing he was in the restaurant made her heart race and her palms sweat. Was she ready to see him with someone else? The beauty about his absence was he wasn't around to remind her of what she was missing. There was some truth to the saying, *Out of sight and out of mind*.

Her phone chimed, and Charlotte's message lit up her screen. *I left what I used on you in the staff bathroom. Touch up before you show up and adjust the twins so they look like they're reaching out for a hand ... shake.*

She laughed as she headed toward the staff bathroom. She'd be happy to touch up her makeup. It was a hot summer day, and she'd probably sweated off most of what

Charlotte applied. In the back of her mind, she heard her mother's voice. *We don't sweat, honey. We glisten.*

When she looked in the mirror, she saw she had glistened all her lipstick off, and her cheeks were slightly pale, but all the rest was as perfect as if Charlotte had just left with her suitcase.

On the shelf above the sink was a bag with her name. She pulled out the tube of lipstick and looked at the name and laughed until she snorted. It was called Pounce on Your Prince Pink. "In my case, they should have named it Punch Your Prince Pink." Thinking about Miles with another woman made her want to feed him a five-finger sandwich. How dare he move on when she was still pining for him.

She gasped. Tilly was right. She'd never gotten over him. And now that he was here, and she'd been so awful to him, he'd moved on.

She applied the lipstick and brushed on more blush. She stared at herself in the mirror. "It's time for operation make him regret he left me." She finger-combed her hair, and when she didn't get the effect she wanted, she bent over, shook her head, and stood, making her appear to have twice the hair she had moments ago. Everything was bigger in Texas, especially hair.

She pasted on a smile she hoped looked genuine and walked into the dining room. It was low-lit, and her eyes had to adjust before she could locate Miles at an out-of-the-way table. His date had her back turned to Em. Her platinum hair caught the glow of the lights, making it look more like spun gold. Miles always liked the blondes, so it didn't surprise her that his date was in that range, but it did surprise her how tiny she was. Blonde and thin and most likely beautiful. A thread of jealousy raced up her spine and wrapped around her heart. The squeeze was the most painful thing she'd felt since her sister's death.

She didn't want to appear interested, so she stayed away from his table for a few minutes, making the rounds but always working her way toward them. When she got there, she braced herself for whatever emotion overtook her, but her heart sank to her sandals when she rounded the table to get a better glance.

"May? Is that you?" She pulled out a chair and took a seat. Her almost-mother-in-law was half her normal size. Her once-full cheeks were sunken, and her skin sallow. Her eyes were ringed with dark circles, making her look exhausted and emaciated.

"Emmaline Brown." May's shaky hand took hers and squeezed. "You haven't aged a day."

"Oh, I've aged thousands of them."

May cupped her cheek. "I sure have missed you, young lady."

"I've been here the whole time." She was no longer jealous but ashamed that she'd let what came between Miles and her keep her from his mother. Her inner voice reminded her that the phone rang on both ends.

The light in May's eyes dimmed. "They were ugly times."

She looked at Miles, who stared at his mother with love. "Why didn't you tell me May was your date?"

He shrugged. "I didn't think you were interested in the intimate details of my life."

"I'm interested in seeing your mom."

"She's been in town since I left, and you haven't been interested until today."

His words were like a jagged, rusty knife piercing her soul. They hurt worse because they were true.

Miles stood. "Would you mind keeping her company while I see what happened to Cormac? He got a call and disappeared, but we wanted to order dinner. I don't want to tire Mom by keeping her out too late."

"No problem. I don't mind keeping her occupied while you're gone."

Miles left, and May didn't give her a chance to say a word. "Give my boy another chance."

Em was taken by the plea. "You want me to take him back, but you never did. Why is that?"

May sat there for a second before a tear slipped from her eye. "I've been letting men decide for me all my life. First, it was my husband, and after he died, Darryl took his place. I didn't want to lose Miles. I'm sure you didn't either, but you and I are the same. We let others decide our paths."

She wanted to refute that statement but couldn't. Everyone around her, from the Fireflies to Cricket, had pointed out that she'd not been the captain of her ship for a long time.

"I don't know, May. How do I go back? There's so much hurt and baggage to get over."

May shook her head. "Honey, you never go back. You go forward. There's nothing in the past but memories. Build a future."

Em raised her hands like she was praising the lord. "Look around. This is my future."

May smiled. "You don't think Miles ended up next door by accident, do you?"

"What do you mean?"

She took one of Em's hands and covered it with her gnarled crepey one. "If Darryl hadn't refused to let Miles stay on the ranch, I would have. He doesn't need to be doting on a dying mother. He needs to be dating you." She smiled. "I prayed that he'd land where he needed to be." Rough, gurgling laughter filled the air. "Who knew it would get him so close to you? Honey, this is divine intervention."

Em thought about everything that had to happen to put Miles next door, and she couldn't argue with May's theory. Someone was at work, but she didn't think it was God. It was Brie and Carter meddling in her life. Karma indeed was a bitch.

Miles and Cormac returned and took their seats, with Cormac to May's left and Miles to Em's right.

"Sorry about that," Cormac said. "My dad thought Uncle Miles kidnapped his mom."

"She's my mom, too," Miles said.

"Dad isn't used to sharing her after all these years. In his mind, everything that has to do with the ranch, including Grandma, belongs to him."

May gave Em an I-told-you-so look. "Well, won't he be surprised."

They all stared at her. "What do you mean, Mom?" Miles asked.

CHAPTER TWELVE

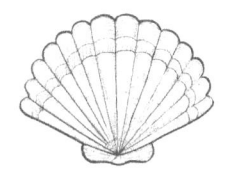

Miles waited for his mom to answer.

May took her napkin and placed it on her lap. "I'm dying, and my last wish is to bring my family back together." She pointed at Cormac. "You did a good job, baby. It took him a long time to get here, but he finally made it."

Miles turned to Cormac. "You looked me up all those years ago because Mom asked you to?"

Cormac frowned. "Well ... okay. If I have to fess up to something, then I think it's only fair that everyone at the table needs to. Isn't it time we cleared the air about lots of stuff?"

Em stood. "I'll leave you so you can have family time."

She turned away, but Miles wasn't letting her go so easily. He grasped her wrist. "Oh, no, you don't. This whole situation includes you. This whole mess is because of you."

"Me?" Her jaw dropped. "I'm not the one who dropped the bomb. You were a one-man laser-guided missile."

"Sit." May's voice was weak but stern.

"Yes, ma'am." She did as she was told because that's how she was raised.

"Good," Miles said. "Because there's a lot of air clearing that needs to be done between you and me."

"That's private."

He chuckled. "Nothing in this town is private. We both know that."

"A lady doesn't air her dirty laundry in public."

"Are we talking about the same lady who stared at my—"

"Don't say it."

Miles loved getting under Emmaline's skin. When she was angry, she was fun, and by the look on her face, things were about to get exciting.

"What was she staring at?" Cormac asked.

Tilly arrived at the table. "Hello, y'all. Since this is a special family reunion dinner, I'll be your server today. The special is steak Oscar, and the day's veggie is zucchini because it's Em's favorite."

"It's not," Em said.

Tilly gave her a questioning look. "No? Weren't you just admiring the zucchini?"

Miles looked between them and knew something was up.

Emmaline opened and closed her mouth several times before her shoulders rolled forward. "I was."

Tilly cleared her throat before continuing with her recommended choices. They all ordered the steak Oscar. Who could pass up a tender filet covered in crab meat and creamy white sauce? Emmaline passed on the meal since she'd already eaten or said she had.

Tilly left, and Cormac took his knife and tapped his water glass to grab everyone's attention. "Since I brought

Grandma, and I seem to be the one taking the brunt of the punishment for being the middleman, I get to speak first." He picked up his glass. "My dad's furious that Uncle Miles is back and has threatened to kick me off the ranch. Someone has to offer me a bed if he does."

May sighed. "It's all my fault. I should have asserted myself years ago, but I grew up in a time where what the husband says goes, so I defaulted to his idiotic sense of justice. If we are having a round of confessions, I'll start. I'm sorry I wasn't strong enough to stand up to your father. He was a mean cuss, and I was afraid to speak my mind. Because of that, I've lost decades with my child, and now I'm on borrowed time, and I realize how stupid I was."

Miles took his mom's hand in his. "It's been said that hindsight is 20/20. If we're confessing, I could have come back five years ago when Dad died, and Cormac looked me up to tell me, but I was bitter and didn't want to deal with it. I figured I didn't owe anything to the people who'd turned their backs on me." He stared directly at Emmaline when he said the words because he got why his parents were furious at him. He'd destroyed their livelihood by telling the truth. But she had wounded him to his marrow with her abandonment. "Now that I'm back, I realize everyone has a different truth, and you aren't wrong in defending yours. We only know what we know, but when we know better, we can do better. I left my job and came back here to make things right. I'm not proud of being the son who ruined his family's life and legacy or the fiancé who destroyed the love of his life's future. If there's a way I can make things better, then tell me." This was no longer about money but character. A person could be richer than Midas, but none of the money mattered if he was a bad person. He planned to redeem his character in the eyes of those who counted, and then he could use his money for good.

All eyes went to Emmaline, who seemed to shrink under their stares. "I will admit to being young, naïve, and fearful of stepping out of my comfort zone." She looked at him. "We had our lives all planned, and our plans got trampled." She sat silently for a moment as if collecting her thoughts. "We were supposed to open a dude ranch where we could use our talents." She pointed to him. "I could have managed the lodging, and you could have run the ranch. That's what you always wanted, but you weren't considered an asset as the second son." She turned to May. "No disrespect, but you treated your sons like Darryl was the heir and Miles was the spare. Do you have any idea how hurtful that is?"

"It's just how it goes. The pressure always falls on the firstborn."

Emmaline shook her head so hard that Miles wondered if she'd need to be seen for a concussion. "Not true. I know this because I suffered the same. Tilly made me see the truth of my life today. I was also the spare. It was my sister who was raised to inherit the resort. I was raised to be her helper. All my life, that pressure to prove myself worthy of a first glance is what motivated me. It also drove me insane. On the outside, I look like a strong and capable woman, but inside I know exactly what I am because it's what everyone has told me my entire life. I'm second rate because I was never their first choice."

Miles's gut twisted. He sat there and replayed her words in his head. He'd never been able to verbalize how he felt, but that was it. He always felt second-rate, and when they tossed him out like he was trash, it confirmed those feelings. He was expendable, whereas Darryl was needed.

Cormac grinned. "That was awesome. Do you feel better?"

"I feel lighter," Miles said. Carrying that around was a heavy burden to bear for years.

"I feel guilty," May said. "There isn't enough time to make up for the hurt I've caused."

Miles squeezed her hand. "Mom, you being here is all I need. To know that you love me and wanted me back is enough."

Emmaline took a sip of her water. "The thing about the past is it's gone. We don't get to change it. It's just what it is. And we aren't promised tomorrow. All we have is the minute we're in. Smart people live in the moment."

The words were lovely, but he knew Emmaline too well. As she sat there, she was thinking about the future.

"You're not going to plan on the slim chance that the travel critic is coming?"

She sat up and frowned. "Smart people plan for the future, too. You can't eat tomorrow if you spend all your money today. Yes, I will plan for the arrival. For all I know, they are sitting in this dining room already."

That was his Emmaline. There were rules for everyone else and rules for her.

"I'll make you a deal," Miles said.

Her brows lifted. "You think you're in a position to negotiate something with me?"

He sat back and laughed. "I have something you want."

Her cheeks turned Hot Tamale red. She moved her hand in a dismissive wave. "Don't flatter yourself."

"What are we talking about?" Cormac asked.

He wanted to say zucchini because he didn't miss the exchange with Tilly, but he wouldn't out Emmaline in front of his family. When he said he had something she wanted, he was referring to his time. "I can help you get everything at your resort ready, just in case."

Emmaline huffed. "In case? The Brown is the only place in town worthy of a stay. You better hope they don't stay at The Kessler because all you've got is Margot, a slobbering dog, and a labor shortage."

"Are you saying you don't want my help?"

"No." She hung her head. "I could use your help. What will it cost me?"

He could have asked for a date or more, but he wanted her to give him those freely. "Stop the labor shortage. I know you did that on purpose. I'm glad because you were right. Cleaning rooms gave me a sense of respect for the people who do it daily. It's hard work. However, if I don't have enough employees, I won't have the time to help you prepare." He could hire his own staff, but he didn't want to overstep his boundaries. Carter and Brie said to let Emmaline handle it all. "Deal?"

"Does that mean you two are back together?" Cormac asked.

"No," Miles said. "It means we've come to a truce. I still care for Emmaline and will help her reach her goals because that's what friends do."

"I'd like something out of this." His mother's voice was weak.

"What do you want, Mom?" Miles asked.

"Family dinners right here, until I can't do them."

"Deal," Miles said.

May cleared her throat. "Darryl too."

"No way," Miles said.

May sighed. "I have one wish before I die, and that's to see my family together again."

What was he supposed to say to that? "Okay. I can give you that."

Tilly delivered their meal. Knowing the next time he dined at The Brown he'd have to see his brother gave him a bitter taste in his mouth. Emmaline excused herself on the premise that she had to help in the dining room, but he didn't see her once while they finished their meal.

He paid, and Darryl was getting out of his truck when they walked outside. He rushed over, screaming, "Who do you think you are?" One second, Miles was standing, and the next, Darryl punched him, and he was on the ground. Knowing a fight would reflect poorly on both resorts, he stood, rubbed his jaw, and then kissed his mom on the cheek.

"See you next week," he said. He looked at Darryl. "I'll see you too."

"Like hell, you will. You stay away from what's mine."

His mother reached up and twisted Darryl's ear until he was bent over and squealing. "Take me home, son. We've got some talking to do." She turned toward Miles. "Love you, and I'll see you Sunday." She walked forward with Darryl begging for her to let him loose, but she didn't until they were at his truck.

He saw a woman with honey-colored hair just before she disappeared inside The Brown boathouse. What was Emmaline up to?

CHAPTER THIRTEEN

She pulled a fifth of whiskey from her pocket and sat on the dock's edge at the outlet to the water. The boathouse was enclosed on three sides and open to the bay, where renters could easily untie their crafts and get on the water quickly.

She untwisted the cap and took a swig. It had been years since she'd snuck a bottle of booze into the boathouse. The last time it happened, she was engaged to a gorgeous cowboy in Willow Bay.

Today she failed to keep her emotions in check. She'd prided herself over the years on always being in control, but his presence threw her off-kilter. How was she supposed to think clearly when he assaulted her senses with his sexiness?

The hinges to the door squeaked, and a large, looming figure walked inside the boathouse and closed the door. There was no need to be alarmed. She recognized his broad shoulders and that walk that some might consider a swagger, but she knew the slight limp came from a horse he tried to break but broke him instead. No one would notice it, but even after all these years, she saw the finer details when it came to Miles.

Her phone buzzed in her pocket, and she stood and took the call because the caller ID said *May McClintock*.

"Hello." It broke her heart to see her so frail at dinner. If May was calling, then something was up.

"It's May, darlin'. I've got a big favor to ask. Can you put Darryl up for a bit?"

In the background, she heard a man's voice say, "I'm not leaving the ranch." Miles sauntered toward her. "I've got one vacancy for a few days."

"That's perfect. He'll be over as soon as he drops me off at the ranch and packs a bag."

"Is there something I should know?" Em asked.

"You already do. My boys are hardheaded and stubborn but redeemable and worthy of love. Sometimes it's tough love. Darryl needs a break." May laughed. "Probably to his head, but maybe it's better served to his ego. I've fired him and booted him from the ranch."

There was a "but mom" in the background before May said thank you and hung up.

When Em finished the call, Miles was there in front of her. In the amber glow of the setting sun, she noticed the swelling and emerging bruise on his jawline.

She reached out to touch it, and he winced. "What the hell happened to you?"

"Family squabble."

Only two family members were in attendance, and she couldn't imagine either of them throwing a punch. Cormac was as sweet as molasses, and May, while in her heyday could have had a powerful right hook, was too weak to punch anything but numbers on her cell phone.

"Who hit you?"

"Darryl. He asked me who I thought I was, and he punched me in the jaw before I could answer. Seeing him for dinner this week will be too soon."

How did she tell Miles that he'd see his brother much sooner than expected? She offered him the bottle.

"Drink up because I'm about to make a bad day worse."

He took the bottle and took several gulps before handing it back. "Worse than getting punched and subjecting myself to weekly family dinners until my mother dies?"

She took a sip and handed the bottle back to him. "Yep. Maybe you should have another drink."

He did as she suggested. "What aren't you telling me?"

"Never mind." She didn't want to ruin his mood. She kicked off her shoes and sat on the edge of the deck, letting her feet dangle over the water. "I haven't been on the water in years." She used to boat all the time as a teen, but it had lost its allure when the boy who kissed her under the stars disappeared.

He took two oars from the nearby stand and untethered a boat. "Let's remedy that." He stepped inside the rowboat, which rocked back and forth. He held out his hand for her to take. "Come on. Let's get away from here for a moment."

She was tempted to take his hand, but alone on a boat with Miles was dangerous for her heart. "It's getting dark."

"Which is perfect. We won't go far. Just to the buoy and back. What do you say?" He thrust his hand forward again. "Don't be a chicken."

He knew exactly what buttons to push. Hell, if he'd used this approach thirty years ago, she probably would have gone with him just to prove she wasn't a coward.

"Fine, but I need to get back soon because I have a lot of planning to do." She took his hand, and he tugged her into the boat. "Wait." She pointed to the dock. "I need my shoes."

"To row?" He shook his head and nodded toward the front bench. "Take a seat, Emmaline." His voice dropped an octave to that low and rough tone that vibrated straight to her core.

Left tingling and speechless, she did what he said, and he maneuvered the boat into open water. The funny thing about the boathouse was that anyone could sneak in from the water and take a boat, but no one did. That was the beauty of living in a small town. And she didn't need to leave to get a taste of the bustle of a big city, because Willow Bay felt like a metropolis during the tourist season. In all her years, she'd never tired of her little corner of the world. She was grateful she hadn't taken Miles's hand that day and went with him, or she wouldn't have what she did now.

Miles stopped rowing as soon as they were a hundred feet from shore. "Do you remember when we used to come out here to watch the stars?" He shifted his body to lay on the bottom of the boat, looking up. He patted the space beside him. "Come down here."

That was a terrible idea. The absolute worst idea she could think of. He was looking at her with those caramel brown eyes with specks of gold that only a setting sun could do justice with. "No. It's uncomfortable and dirty."

"All these years later, you still have the same argument." He lifted and took off his shirt and placed it beside him. "Now come join me. Let's watch the stars come out."

The sun settled like a fireball being eaten by the ocean, and the night would be upon them within minutes. Heart and head battled, but her heart won. She shimmed down to the bottom of the boat and tried to get comfortable. After fidgeting for a few minutes, he pulled her on top of his body, just like he used to do, with her back side nestled against his front side. Miles would suffer through the discomfort of the wood planking poking his back, and she would enjoy his soft and hard parts under her. When she thought about the hard parts, all kinds of feelings emerged as she wormed and wiggled on top of him.

"Would you stay still?"

"I can't. There's something hard poking me in my thigh." She shifted again, but it was still there.

Miles chuckled. "He's just happy to see you."

She gasped. "Miles McClintock, are you for real?"

He reached between them. "Nope." A few seconds later, he yanked out his keyring. "Just my keys."

The teenage girl who lived inside her heart wanted him to respond the way he used to, the way he did earlier when he let his pants drop and she stared at him for an embarrassingly long time. She acted like she hadn't seen one of those in a lifetime. She hadn't, but she wasn't about to confess that.

"Tell me about the last thirty years," she said.

He shifted again, so her head was on his shoulder, and she was cradled half on and off him with one hand cupping her hip and one of her legs flung over both of his. She didn't have much view of the stars, but what she saw was far better. Staring at his profile, she couldn't understand how he'd aged and become better while she'd just gotten old. Life was unfair.

"Here's the short version. Work. Work. More work. There was some schooling in there too. I moved around, and each time I went to another state, I had to retest to get my license for that state."

"But you covered as an EMT here. Did you do that legally?"

His hand moved lower when she started to slide off him until he gripped her bottom.

"Emmaline, I'm surprised you feel compelled to ask me that. You know me. I'm a rule follower. By the way, I'm not an EMT. I'm a paramedic, and I am licensed in this state. When I left Willow Bay, I did my training in Dallas and worked there for some time."

"What's the difference?"

"I can do more as a paramedic."

"Oh." That made sense because Miles was always an overachiever. Miles finished it in a day if his father wanted something done in a week. He could brand an entire herd in half the time Darryl could. She knew because she'd watched him. "What made you leave Dallas?"

"What I was looking for wasn't there."

The wind shifted, and a cool breeze danced across her skin. Or that's what she blamed for the sensitive gooseflesh prickling against her clothes. Did she dare ask what he was looking for, or did she let it go? She'd punch him in his other side of his jaw if he said something stupid like clarity. Common sense wasn't her friend today, and she couldn't help herself from asking. "What were you looking for?" No matter what answer he offered, she'd have to keep her fists to herself since she'd asked.

When he scooted sideways, she slid down to the boat's hull, and Miles turned to face her. "I've been looking for something to fill the emptiness you left behind when you didn't want me anymore."

Her heart twisted, and a sharp, piercing pain in her chest convinced her he'd ripped it apart with his words. Her instinct was to lash out and blame him, but she couldn't because he was right, she'd turned her back on him.

"I'm so sorry, Miles. I was young and stupid and under the influence."

He lifted on an elbow. "You were drunk?"

"I wish. It would have numbed the pain of losing you. No, I was still under the impression that I could win my parents over. For whatever reason, their approval was so important to me." They were dead, and she was still trying to make them proud. Charlotte told her she needed therapy, but hers came in a whole pie, a tub of ice cream, and a talk with Cricket, the wisest woman she knew.

"I understand. Imagine that day for a second. I'm trying to do right by everyone. I don't want you to marry into a family that will ruin your reputation for life. I don't want your father investing in cattle that aren't what they seem. It was like paying for Wagyu and getting top sirloin. Then there was us, and I didn't want you marrying a man who knew something was wrong and did nothing about it. That day, I did what was right and lost everything."

She felt like such a fool. "If you had to do it all over again, would you do the same thing?"

He reached forward and twisted a lock of her hair around his finger. She could see his mind moving through all the scenarios as the golden specks in his eyes shifted with his thoughts. Miles could never get away with much because his eyes were so expressive. He never had a great poker face, but she didn't know what he'd say this time.

"I've thought about that a lot." He cupped her cheek. "I hated what happened to us, but maybe it was a good thing. We weren't ready for the love we deserved, and I don't think we knew how to give the love we needed. So, to answer your question, yes, I would have done the same thing because when we leave this world, all we leave behind are memories, and I'd rather be known as a man with integrity." His thumb brushed her cheek. "What about you?"

She reached out and laid her hand on his hip. It didn't stay there long as the pull to know whether the hair on his chest was soft or course drew her to him. Those tiny hairs sprouting all those years ago were both, and she loved how her fingers felt as she brushed her fingertips through them.

"I regret not going away with you, but I don't regret staying."

"You can't have it both ways."

"By staying, I ended up with The Brown. That's what I wanted all along."

"You're wrong." They were close enough for his breath to tickle her cheek. For several seconds his gaze lingered on her mouth until he leaned in and touched his lips to hers. "Let me remind you of what you wanted." She barely had time to take a breath before his mouth covered hers. When her lips parted for a sigh, his tongue entered. He tasted like sweet tea and passion.

A hundred memories flooded her senses, and all those past feelings of love and desire came rushing back. She moved closer until their bodies were connected from lips to toes. Her endorphin-infused blood raced through her veins. Everything was perfect: his body's warmth, his tongue's velvety texture, and his lips' satiny softness. Then there were his hands on her body, sliding up. It was so perfect that she heard angels sing.

He pulled away, breaking the spell, and she realized her phone was ringing.

"Don't answer that," he said breathlessly.

She pulled her phone from her pocket and saw it was The Brown. "I have to." She gave him another peck before she answered.

"What's up?" The receptionist told her a demanding guest was waiting in the lobby. "I'll be right there."

She hung up and looked at Miles. "I'm sorry, but I have to go. A problem just arrived."

He rose, took his seat, and picked up the oars. "A problem? What kind of problem?"

She took her seat while he rowed them toward shore. "It's not a what as much as a who. Do you remember when I said there was probably something you should know?"

"Yes." He rowed harder, and they arrived at the dock quickly. "Just tell me."

"May kicked Darryl off the ranch, and I've got the only place in town to stay." She cleared her throat. "Not true. You've got the only vacancy, so Darryl is staying at The Kessler for a few days."

"No way!" He moved the boat into its space.

"It's already done. I couldn't say no to your mom." She climbed out before the boat came to a complete stop, grabbed her shoes, and took off, running toward the front desk.

"Emmaline," he called after her. "What we started isn't finished."

She laughed as she pushed through the door. "I know, but do you think this is wise?"

CHAPTER FOURTEEN

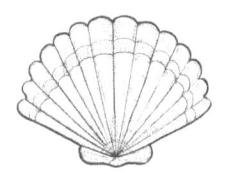

He tied up the rowboat and chased after her. With Emmaline, nothing was easy, but that kiss reminded him that it was worth it. The single kiss told him time hadn't changed how they responded to each other. They might be fire and ice, but he'd be damned if he could stay away from her. He'd tried for decades, and all he got from his absence was misery and loneliness.

He heard yelling coming from inside as he approached.

"I'm not staying anywhere near my brother," Darryl said.

Miles walked in the door and was about to say something when Emmaline looked up at him and held up her hand, indicating that she had it under control.

"For a man with no place to stay, you're being quite demanding. Miles has the only vacancy in town. Take it or leave it."

"What do you mean, Miles has the only vacancy in town?" Darryl asked.

She looked between them. "He's the manager of The Kessler."

Darryl narrowed his eyes. "Then why did I have to come here for my reservation?"

She shrugged. "We are joining forces while my niece and nephew are on their honeymoon. The Kessler isn't fully staffed." She rubbed her chin. "May said you need a job, too. We can help with that."

Darryl rolled his eyes and turned to face Miles. "Mom won't keep me away from the ranch for too long. She's too sick to deal with it."

Miles chuckled. "I'm sure Cormac can handle the chickens and the few head of cattle you've got. I'd prepare for the long haul."

"I'm not staying with you," Darryl said.

"You're right. I'm staying in a house. The most I can offer is a room with a bed and a bathroom. It's got clean linens, cable, and a Keurig coffee machine."

Emmaline smiled. "I'll leave you to figure out the details. Remember, no fighting on the premises, and quiet hour begins at ten." She looked around the lobby. "If you break it, you buy it. You should know that my family has excellent taste." She stared at Miles while she said that last sentence. "I'm known for quality choices." She walked to the door, stopped, and turned to Darryl. "They say what goes around comes around. Maybe you should have been nicer to Miles when he needed you."

Darryl snorted. "Maybe you should have."

She nodded. "I definitely should have."

She stood in front of Miles. "The Kessler is yours to operate, and you can turn him away, but he needs you. You can repeat history and banish your brother from the property or turn the other cheek and be a good human. The choice is yours."

"I always try to be a good human, but Darryl isn't ever going to change."

She looked over her shoulder and then back to him. "You told me all we leave is memories. What memories will you leave, Miles?" She walked away and disappeared around the corner to her house.

When he returned to The Brown's front desk, Darryl was standing there looking like someone had stolen his tricycle. "What's it going to be?"

Darryl marched over with his fist in the air. "I have a mind to knock that smug smile from your face. What did you say to Mom to get her to kick me off the ranch?"

"You heard Emmaline. No violence. I gave you the first one for free, but you touch me again, and I'll make sure you never raise that fist again." Staring at his brother was like looking at a twin of his father. "Do you want the room or not?"

Darryl caved in front of him. "It's not like I have a choice. Unless I want to sleep in my truck."

"Marybeth might let you stay. That's where I landed when you kicked me off the ranch this time." He couldn't believe his brother could be so heartless. Their mother was dying, and he made him leave.

Darryl shook his head. "I stopped by the church first, and she's already got a guest."

"It would seem that you owe me an apology. Once I get that, I'll get you a room."

"It will be a wintry day in hell before I apologize."

"Enjoy your night in the truck." He walked out the door of The Brown and moved toward his place. He had painting to do. "Don't park your vehicle on resort property, or you'll be towed."

"That's right," Darryl taunted. "Walk away. It's what you do best."

He stopped and spun around to face him. "When you're twisting your tale, don't forget I wasn't the one stealing from everyone."

Darryl's hands fisted at his sides as he moved closer, but he kept them tightly pressed to his jeans. "You stole from me. You ruined my life."

"That was never my intention, and I apologize because you were another innocent victim in our father's scheme to steal from those buying his cattle."

Darryl stood taller. "You don't think I knew? I was completely aware of what he was doing, and it was brilliant until you shouted it to the world. We were making bank on our cattle sales."

"You were hurting those who were helping you. You took advantage of the people who put food on our table." Hearing that Darryl knew about the fraud only made it worse. He was exactly like their father, and nothing was redeemable.

"My wife left me after we settled all the lawsuits. There wasn't enough left to maintain the life she wanted to live."

In that way, they weren't much different. Emmaline chose security over love, too. He should be furious with her, but he wasn't. He'd had a lot of time to reflect on what she'd done and what he'd done. Two wrongs never made a right. He meant it when he said their breakup was probably for the best. They'd both had a long time to reflect and grow as people.

"Next time, choose someone who loves you for who you are and not the material things you can offer. I think that a personality is something you have to offer someone." He was glad he decided not to tell anyone about his lottery win.

The people around him were there for the right reasons. As far as anyone was concerned, he was a resort manager, not some guy with twenty-two million dollars in multiple bank accounts.

"Seems to me you would benefit from your own advice. Emmaline wouldn't even marry you."

"Years ago, that might have had the painful impact you were looking for, but I'm immune to your form of torture. As for Emmaline ... she made a smart decision, or her father did. They sent me away, but I grew up and became a better man. It will be for all the right reasons when I win her back."

"Win her back?" Darryl laughed. "Hell will freeze over before that happens."

"Better get your coat. I feel a storm coming our way." He continued toward the house. "Have a good night, Darryl."

Ollie was waiting by the door when he entered. Next to him was a pile of left shoes.

"What have you been up to?" The dog laid down and covered his snout with his paws. "Where did you get these?"

When he adopted Ollie from the pound, his original name was Houdini because the previous owner swore he could walk through walls. Miles had seen none of that behavior until this moment. He looked at the pile of shoes and saw everything from children's sandals to an adult bunny slipper. Somehow Ollie had escaped, and while he was having dinner, his dog was collecting trophies.

"You're a kleptomaniac. What am I going to do with you?"

He knew exactly what he had to do tonight. He needed to hide the evidence. He was finally on Emmaline's good side, and he wasn't letting his thieving dog change that.

He gathered the half dozen shoes and walked out the door. He'd plant a few around the resort, put a couple in lost and found at The Kessler, and leave the next two on the steps of The Brown for someone else to find.

He felt like a burglar, tiptoeing through the grounds, and surreptitiously hiding Ollie's treasures. As he walked back, the culprit rushed over with his tail wagging.

"How did you get out of the house?" He swore he'd shut the door but supposed he might have left it open a tad. "You need to be good because we're a team, and if one of us gets kicked off the premises, we both have to go. That means no Emmaline for me and no lost and found rejects for you." He looked into Ollie's eyes and somehow knew the dog understood him. "You want to help me paint?"

Ollie's bark said it all. He was game for anything as long as they were together.

CHAPTER FIFTEEN

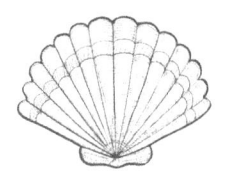

Emmaline showed up at Miles's place at six-thirty in the morning with a plate of warm mini quiche and two cups of coffee. With no free hands, she kicked the door several times, hoping the muted thump would wake him. Way back when, he slept like the dead, but so had she, and nowadays, she woke to the slightest sound.

The loud woof on the other side meant Ollie was a light sleeper or had a keen sense of smell and picked up on the quiche. After several minutes, she heard Miles talking to the dog like a human, asking him who could be on the other side, and if they were waking him at the crack of dawn, they'd better have coffee.

When he opened the door, she smiled. "Room service." She stared at the dog, hoping her stern look kept him at bay.

When she glanced at Miles, she found him shirtless with zipped but unbuttoned jeans that appeared to hang precariously on his hips. Miles was a handsome man, and she didn't imagine he'd spent a lot of mornings waking up alone. Just the thought made her heart ache.

"Now, this is the best wake-up call I've had in a long time," he said

"I would have thought you'd wake up to women on the regular. Breakfast in bed and kisses and all that." She moved past him and went straight to the kitchen, where she freed her hands by setting everything on the table. She opened several cupboards before she found small plates and took one out for him.

"I get slobbery ones daily from Ollie, but he's not much of a snuggler." He moved to the table and sat, where she joined him. He picked up a cup of coffee and tested it for heat. When he found it drinkable, he closed his eyes and drank deeply. A rumbling sound of satisfaction slipped from his lips, and she swore it headed straight for her core. "Do you remember how nice it was to spoon?" He dug into the mini quiche, popping a whole one into his mouth.

"I remember." She sipped her coffee and stared at him, recalling how his lips made her burn with passion. She was half grateful and mostly annoyed that Darryl showed up when things were getting good on the water last night. "I also remember you snore."

He chuckled. "Have you ever heard of hertz healing sounds? My snore is perfectly tuned to 417 Hz, which reduces stress. Sleeping with me is like having a personal Zen master."

"Sleeping with you is like bedding a freight train."

He smiled. "I'll take that. When I think of trains, I think about endurance and those long-haul trips. Some of them are so long they—"

She held up her hand. "I get it." She touched her cheek, hoping the heat didn't show in a blush. Since when did she blush at sexual innuendo? "I didn't come to talk about your train."

"I think you did. You're the one who brought it up." He picked up another quiche and popped it into his mouth. He chewed and swallowed and pointed to her. "You're not having any?"

"I ate an hour ago. I let you sleep in." She woke at four-thirty, and it killed her to wait until six-thirty to knock on his door. It seemed a reasonable time, and she brought him breakfast, which she considered payment for the early hour. "The birds have been up since four."

He shook his head. "I'm not a bird. Besides, I was up until midnight painting the living room."

She lifted her nose and inhaled. There was a hint of something sitting in the air, but it didn't smell like paint. "All I smell is dog breath and quiche." She glanced down at Ollie, who sat obediently beside her, staring at her shoes and drooling. "You are a good boy. You didn't plow me over today when I arrived."

"Because you gave him the stink eye." Miles finished the last quiche and leaned back to pat his stomach. A fine hairline led her eyes to his jeans button and zipper.

"What brings you here, Emmaline? I'm sure you didn't come to help me dress for the day again. If you did, let's do it."

Her roaming eyes snapped up to meet his mirth-filled ones. "I came to talk about the plan. You know, the one we made last night while dining with your mother. The one where you help me prepare for the travel critic."

"Right ... the plan. Is The Kessler fully staffed today? If it isn't, I can't help you."

"You have a full staff." She hated to admit she'd short-handed him, but it was a good lesson. Running a resort wasn't easy, and sometimes getting his hands dirty would be necessary.

"I knew you shortchanged me. Now that we're over that, what if the critic is already here?"

She pulled a paper from her back pocket. "Here are The Brown and Kessler guests. I've looked them up online, and no one is affiliated with a travel agency, airline, magazine, or anything."

"I imagine they keep that under wraps since these things are done on the sly." He rubbed his chin. "Wouldn't you rather they judged the resort on how things ran rather than how they are supposed to run?"

She snorted with indignation. "The Brown is perfect as is, and I'm sure we could do nothing, and it would get stellar reviews, but don't you understand? This is the opportunity my father was always waiting for; after he passed, it was what my sister coveted. Do you know what getting a five-star review from a professional traveler means to us?"

"Don't you mean you? There is no us in your equation. Everyone you mentioned is dead."

"You'll never get it, but I'll try to explain. Getting that five-star review means I was good enough. After all those years when my father didn't choose me, a great review will prove he was wrong. I can run the resort."

He sighed. "Okay, let's get that five-star review, but remember, you don't have to prove anything to anyone. We all know you're capable. I've always believed in you." He stood. "You coming to watch me dress, or do you want me to meet you somewhere?" He didn't wait for her answer and walked away.

She had no choice but to follow him, or that's what she told herself. Once at his room, which was Carter's old room, she walked inside and turned her back while he dropped his jeans and reached for another pair. She knew exactly what he was doing and missed none of it because she gawked at him in the mirror's reflection. It was hard to admit, but she had truly missed him. There was a saying, *you don't know what you missed until it's gone.* But it should be, *You don't know what you missed until it left, came back, and stood in front of you naked.*

"You don't have to be shy," he said. "You've seen it all before." He looked at her back, and she knew exactly when he figured out she'd been watching him in the mirror. "Turn around, Emmaline. I've never known you to be a wilting flower. If you want to look, then look."

She whipped around. "I didn't come in here to ogle."

He pulled on his pants and tucked himself gently inside before zipping and buttoning. "You could have fooled me. If watching me get dressed wasn't on your agenda, then what was?"

She knew she'd be distracted until he was fully clothed, so she reached for the Kessler logo shirts he had stacked on the dresser behind her and tossed him one. Once he was dressed, she said, "I wanted to make sure we were on the same page, and I was curious about Darryl and how it all turned out. I didn't see his truck in the parking lot this morning."

"He refused to stay."

"Can we rent the room?" There was nothing like full occupancy to impress a critic. And while she didn't want to accept that they could stay at The Kessler, she had to consider the possibility.

"I think he'll be back. My mom won't give in and let him return to the ranch, and there isn't any place in town to stay."

He pulled on his boots and spritzed himself with his cologne. It seemed to swirl around her like a hug.

"I'm sure Marybeth can put him up."

He brushed her arm as he moved past to get his wallet and comb from the dresser. "He tried that before he came here. She's filled up too. It would seem I vacated her place at the perfect time."

"Speaking of that. Who approached whom about you working here? You or Carter?"

"It was me. I asked Cormac to set up a meeting. I knew Carter's father, Cyrus, had passed away. Through the grapevine, I'd heard Carter was back in town. Rumors were swirling about him and Brie. Marybeth isn't known for her secret-keeping skills. The hardest thing to comprehend was how they'd grown from babies to the adults they are today. So much happened while I was away."

"Life doesn't stop. It just continues to drone on. But why The Kessler?" She followed him back to the kitchen, where he cleaned the table and washed the dish he'd used. She liked that he was tidy. Her granny used to say cleanliness was next to godliness. In her mind, keeping things tidy kept the roaches away.

"Over the years, I'd saved a little money and figured if Carter wasn't going to stay, maybe he'd—"

"Let you manage it?"

"Something like that."

"But you knew it would put you in direct contact with me."

He approached her until they were a breath apart. "I've never been afraid of you, Emmaline." He exhaled, and his breath caressed her lips. "In all this time, my only fear was of you rejecting me, and that happened years ago, and I survived. Being here doesn't affect me nearly as much as you." He brushed his lips across hers and pulled back, but she wasn't letting him get away so easily.

Were his words designed to hurt? She didn't think so

because, if she were honest, Miles never had a mean bone in his body. It was one thing she'd loved about him. He was a man of integrity and kindness, but right now, he was lying, and she was going to prove it.

"No? Not affected at all, huh?" She placed her hand on his chest, moved it to his stomach, and then lower. She kissed his neck. When her palm dropped to his zipper, she cupped him. He was definitely affected by her presence. She stood back and smiled. "I've never known you to be a liar." She turned and walked toward the door. In the living room, she looked at the paint. "You were right. You are a man who pays attention to the details." She sighed as she walked to the door. "Shall we?"

CHAPTER SIXTEEN

He tapped his leg, and Ollie followed him out the door.

"He's not coming," Emmaline said.

Would he have to fight Emmaline at every turn? "He is." He didn't want to tell her that if they left him behind, he'd find a way out. "I'm his support human, and he needs me." The door was closed when they returned to the house last night. The best Miles could figure was Ollie could open doors and, since he had never left him behind, Ollie never had to. Even when he was a paramedic, he made sure Ollie was occupied. He spent a lot of money on doggie daycare, because he felt having an animal was like having a child. He had a responsibility to make sure Ollie was cared for.

"He's a nuisance." She moved toward the dock while they followed.

"If you want me, he's part of the deal." He ruffled the top of Ollie's head. "Who's a good boy?"

"Not him. I'm still nursing a bruise on my backside from the day he knocked me over."

"I'm happy to rub it for you. Arnica works wonders on bruises. I'll pick up some when I'm in town."

"When are you going to town? Do you have another date?" They arrived at the boathouse, and she unlocked the door.

"Are you jealous?" He loved that she was. She could deny it all she wanted, but a woman didn't look at him like Emmaline did and not have feelings. She stared at him like a starving man staring at a steak.

She glanced at Ollie and then at him. "Jealous?" She dismissed that notion with a wave of her hand. "No, I've seen the company you keep. They're four-legged slobbering furballs or frail older women."

"You forced me to spend the day with Margot. She only felt me up twice and proposed once."

Emmaline gasped. "She didn't."

"Okay, she didn't propose."

She shook her head. "That girl needs a mother."

"Or a spanking," he said.

"I'm fairly certain she'd like that." Emmaline walked to the boat they'd rowed last night. She climbed in and felt around until she came up with the bottle of booze. "Here it is."

"It's a little early to hit the bottle, no?"

She tucked it in her back pocket. "We can't leave things like this in the boat. There are children present."

He wanted to say that she'd left it in the boat, but he didn't. "Is that the only reason we're in the boathouse?" He moved down the decking, looking at the boats bobbing as the tide rolled in. Today's forecast was for strong winds, which hopefully meant she'd close the boathouse. It wasn't safe to let people in the water when it was rough.

"No." She pointed to the rafters. "Hugh is too old to

climb to get the cobwebs down. With the boathouse closed for weather, I thought it's a good place for us to start."

He returned to her. "If you wanted to be alone in the boathouse together, all you had to do was say so."

"Are you daft? This isn't about us. This is about getting the resort five-star ready." She moved past him and pointed out all the things she wanted done. It was a full day's work, but he was happy to do it if it meant they'd spend the day together. "I'll check in with you later."

"Whoa, wait a minute. You said you wanted me to help you get the resort ready. I assumed you meant we were working as a team."

She rubbed her temples and sighed. "You and I know that if we are together, we aren't getting much done. I'll be distracted by the view, and you'll…"

"I'll what?"

"Want to kiss me again?"

Was that hope he saw in her eyes? "I agree. So … let's work on a reward system. If we get the boathouse clean, I get to kiss you."

She cocked her head. "And what do I get?"

He wanted to roll his eyes, but he'd play along. "As if the kiss wasn't enough."

"That's what you want, but what's my reward?"

He smiled. "I'll kiss you shirtless."

Emmaline's smile always warmed him, but right then, it hit him like the sun's rays on a cloudless day. "Deal. Let's get to work."

Three hours later, every cobweb was gone. They stood looking at their accomplishment. It felt good to complete something with Emmaline. This was the dream way back when. They were always good together and should have been running their own resort by now, but he'd been too honest. Never in his life did he think honesty would dump a load of coal on his diamond dreams.

"What now?" he asked.

She wiped a bead of sweat from her brow. "I think this is where you kiss me." He leaned in, but she placed her hand on his chest. "Shirtless."

He turned and walked away.

"You're leaving?"

There was so much disbelief in her voice that he wanted to laugh. In what world would he leave her when she wanted him? That universe didn't exist. He got to the door, locked it, and returned.

"I don't want any distractions because when I kiss you, I'm going to kiss you senseless." He grabbed the hem of his shirt and pulled it over his head. Seeing her eyes light up made every cobweb he removed worth it. Even the one he had to climb into the rafters to get. "All I want is you, Emmaline."

She fell into him and placed her head on his chest. She would never be a woman who surrendered, but this was close.

"I've missed you, Miles."

"I'm here, sweetheart." He backed her up until he was at the blanket shelf. Thankfully, they hadn't stopped providing them to boaters who might get chilly on the water. While he nuzzled her neck, he pulled several free. "Unless you have other plans, I plan to kiss you for a while." He kissed her quickly before he bit her lower lip and sucked it into his mouth. Her groan was his undoing, or maybe it was her hands at his back, pulling him closer. If he got any closer, he'd be inside her; that was precisely where he wanted to be.

He didn't want to interrupt what was happening, only enhance it, so he stepped back and haphazardly tossed the blankets on the decking before he invited her to join him.

Like the teens they once were, they kissed and felt and fondled until they were breathless. She was no longer the twenty-year-old he'd wanted to marry. She was more.

"I don't want to stop," he said. "Do you remember the first time we made love?"

She tugged at the button of his jeans while he unbuttoned her shirt. He wanted to grip both sides and tear it open, but he painstakingly unbuttoned it and let it fall open and looked at her lacy pink bra. It was so dainty and feminine and so Emmaline. On the outside, she was tough as nails, but inside she was as fragile as the lace before him.

Hard nipples pressed against the delicate fabric, and he pulled a tightened bud into his mouth, feeling the material's texture against his tongue.

She writhed and moaned beside him while he tugged at the button of her jeans. "I want this, Emmaline. I want us." He didn't come back to Willow Bay for her, but he'd be damned if he'd be here and not win her back. "I'm all-in, baby. Are you in?"

She laughed. "You're not in, but you better be soon. I've waited too long."

He wanted to know how long she'd waited. When was her last love affair? Who was it with? Thinking about her with anyone else made his blood burn, not angry, but in a primal caveman way.

He rolled over and kneeled between her legs. With a

few tugs, he removed her pants while she shrugged off her shirt. She lay there in her lace and beauty, and all he could do was stare. "Beautiful. Damn, you haven't changed a bit."

"Liar, but I like that lie." She reached up to help him with his jeans. "Too many clothes, cowboy."

That had always been her line back then, and all he said was, "Yes, ma'am." Today he said nothing. He stood, kicked off his boots, and dropped his pants. Ollie ran over, stole his left boot, and disappeared into the shadows.

As he leaned over her, he looked into her eyes. There were so many emotions present, but what stood out the most was love. Could she love him again? He promised to make her try.

When he entered her, thirty years disappeared, and the woman he'd always loved was beneath him, giving as much as she took. His body remembered hers, and instinct took over. Her hands found his back, and they moved in a rhythm that was their own. She demanded, and he gave. She offered, and he took. They spent the next thirty minutes loving and pleasing each other. He paid attention to those details she spoke of, and once she'd found her release, he settled into a rhythm and raced after his. When they were finished, he held her in his arms. No words needed to be exchanged. Their bodies had done all the talking. Emmaline was his, and he was hers. It was the way it was supposed to be all along.

She moved away from him, and he knew their moment was over.

"That was—"

"If you say anything other than perfect, then I'll call you out for lying," he said.

She stood and looked around for her clothes. "It was just as I remembered. How is that possible? We've both changed." She put on her underwear and bra and stepped into her jeans.

He hopped up and took her in his arms. "We've gotten older, but have we changed? I don't think so. Inside, I'm still the cowboy you fell in love with, and you're still Emmaline, the girl who stole my heart."

She smiled and then shook her head. "I'm not the same."

He wrapped his arms around her. "Okay, if you say so, but I just made love to you, and it felt the same as it did all those years ago. It was perfect." He kissed her and stood back. "I still love you. I always have."

She pressed her head against his chest. "I don't want to love you, Miles, but I can't help myself. I'm scared you'll break my heart again."

He held her close. "And I'm scared you'll push me away." He kissed the top of her head. "Let's agree to take it one day at a time."

She looked at him. "Or ... one project. You want to do that again after we clean all the loungers and tables?"

"Can't someone else do that, and we go straight for the reward?" He laughed. "I feel like delegating should be rewarded as well."

"I like how you think, but everyone is busy, and Hugh can't get it all done."

"I'm surprised he's still here."

She shrugged. "I don't have the heart to let him go. It's important for people to feel like they belong."

"And his wife has an unquenchable QVC habit."

"How do you know?"

"He told me when I helped him clean out the fire pit."

They finished dressing and gathered the blankets. "One day, I'll have to let him go. He gets more forgetful each day and it takes him four times as long to do anything as anyone else, but today is not the day."

When he couldn't find his left boot, he called Ollie, who trotted over, carrying it in his mouth. "Thanks, boy." He pulled his boot on and petted Ollie's head.

"He never chews them?"

"No, he's a lover, not a chewer."

They exited the boathouse and locked the door behind them.

"There you are," Margot yelled from the porch of The Kessler. "We've got a problem."

Emmaline rose on tiptoes and kissed him. "I'll take these to the laundry and meet you on the beach in ten minutes?"

"I'll be there."

They parted on the cement path. Whatever problem was waiting for him, it better not take over ten minutes because he didn't want to be away from her for that long.

When he and Ollie entered the lobby, he saw the problem—Darryl.

Margot pointed to him. "He says the last available room is his, and he's not paying. I told him that he didn't have a room if he didn't have money. We aren't a charity."

A family of four walked into the lobby and stood on the other side of the desk. Since Margot wasn't paying attention, he stepped in.

"Good morning. My name is Miles, and I'm the manager here. Can I help you?"

"Towels," the woman said. She was short on words and patience.

"Certainly." He walked behind the counter and grabbed four. "It'll be windy and overcast, but keep sunscreen on. I've gotten my worst burns on a cloudy day." Next to the towels was a box of sunscreen packets. He picked up a handful and set them on the towels before handing them to the woman. "If you haven't had breakfast, I can vouch for the mini-quiche."

The woman's icy demeanor melted. "Can you have someone send that and orange juice out to us?"

"I can do that."

"Perfect."

He had to agree. This day was perfect. Then he looked at his brother and thought, almost.

As soon as the family was gone, he turned to Margot. "He's family, and he can stay in the room."

"But..."

Miles held up his hand. "If he doesn't have money, he'll work for his room and board."

"I'm not working here," Darryl said.

Miles looked at his brother's eyes, shadowed by a lack of sleep. His hair was mussed, and his clothes wrinkled.

"How was last night in your truck?" As his brother's shoulders folded forward, he knew he'd won this battle, but there would be many more.

"He's not taking my job," Margot said.

"Margot, do your job and order that family breakfast delivered to the beach."

"We don't do that."

"We do now. The Kessler is a full-service resort. If someone wants a pie from Cricket's, we'll get it. If they want their toes rubbed with blueberry preserves, find a pedicurist willing to do it."

"That's not me," Darryl said. "I don't like feet."

"Do you think you're in a position to tell me what you will or won't do?"

CHAPTER SEVENTEEN

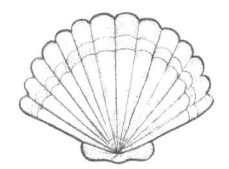

After waiting for what seemed like a lifetime for Miles, Em searched for him and found him in the lobby of The Kessler in what looked like a standoff with Darryl. Both men had that immovable cement wall stance.

"What's up?" she asked as she walked inside the door.

Darryl pointed at Miles. "He's under the mistaken impression that I'm going to work for my room and board."

She always considered that a funny saying. When did the word board become meals? She let go of that thought and faced the situation in front of her. Darryl was red-faced and had his hands fisted at his sides. Miles looked as cool and sweet as a Dreamsicle.

"Can you pay for your room?"

"No, I've got no money." He nodded toward his brother. "I've been flat broke since he left."

There were a lot of things Em didn't like. She didn't like lima beans, leftovers, or liars, but mostly she loathed people who refused to help themselves.

"What have you done to improve yourself and your situation in the last three decades?"

He gave her a strange, crinkled-nose look. It was the same expression her mother had when she opened the milk carton and found it spoiled.

"I bought chickens."

"Chickens are a far cry from cattle." She held up her hand before he could say another word. "I know you blame him for that, but that was your daddy's fault. He'd been blowin' smoke up people's asses for years. Stealing from the locals is like stealing from family. It isn't right and shouldn't be done. Stop blaming your brother for your lack of success. My grandma always used to say if you plant a butter bean, don't be expecting an apple tree to grow. If you want something to change, then do something different." She pointed to Margot. "Get him a shirt."

Margot bolted for the storage closet.

"You're making me work?" Darryl asked.

"There are two ways you stay here. You either pay for your room, or you work for your room. Since you can't pay for it, I assume you'll take option two."

Margot came back and held out two shirts. "Large or extra-large?"

Darryl swiped the extra-large. "Fine, but I'm not working for him."

Em sighed. "You are if you want to stay here. He runs The Kessler. What he says goes. Take it or leave it." She turned and smiled at Miles, and he stared at her like she'd grown a third eye. He probably wasn't expecting her full support, but if he was going to run The Kessler, then she had to let him run The Kessler. "Are we still working on the loungers?"

Miles nodded. "Give me a few minutes to get Darryl situated, and I'll be out."

Em stuck around for an extra minute to ensure fists

didn't fly, and when she was certain Darryl had accepted his fate, she walked outside. It was a lovely day, despite the wind and cooler temperatures. The beach filled up with guests who refused to give up a day on the sand. She couldn't blame them. Life was busy and complicated and stressful, but even a windy day on the beach was better than a day in the office.

Miles and Darryl walked past her to The Kessler boathouse, and she was happy to see Miles put him to work in a place where he wouldn't come into contact with guests. There was nothing worse for business than an unhappy employee, and while Darryl wasn't technically an employee, wearing a Kessler T-shirt would make him appear so. His attitude would be bad for business.

Knowing Miles would be a while longer, she headed to the kitchen and Tilly. As soon as she entered, Tilly moved from behind the line and came to the table.

"Is that a glow I see on your face?"

The mention of a glow heated Em's cheeks and gave her away. She pulled Tilly to the corner. "Oh my God. It was amazing."

"I want all the details." Tilly moved to the coffeepot on the nearby sideboard and measured the grounds. While they put K-Cups in the rooms, the coffee from the kitchen was always freshly brewed and contained chicory, which gave it that rich and slightly bitter taste you only got from southern-brewed coffee.

"I don't have time for the details now because we have a cleaning date."

Tilly stopped with a scoop of grounds in the air. "A cleaning date? That man is getting off cheap, or you're obsessed with the idea of the critic and can't see what's right in front of you. Forget the cleaning and focus. You've got a hot man who wants you. No review is worth giving that man up for."

"I'm not obsessed. Besides, why can't I have both?"

"You two could be in your room getting on that glow again, but you're going to clean? Your priorities are skewed." She dumped the grounds into the filter and pressed the start button. "Seriously, didn't you learn anything from the past?"

"Girl, we aren't twenty anymore. While getting my glow on again sounds amazing in theory, I'm fairly certain we aren't up to a repeat so soon."

"Fine, but if that man were mine…"

Em giggled. "Honey, you'd be in traction." She leaned toward Tilly and whispered, "I might need a massage later. He threw down blankets and made love to me in the boathouse."

"Some things never change."

"No, they don't. It was just as good as I remembered."

"Don't rub it in." She filled up three cups and handed Em two. "Sounds like you both need this. There's nothing like a little caffeine to ignite that get-up-and-go."

Em had never known Tilly to date. "When was the last time you…"

"David Hasselhoff."

"*The* David Hasselhoff?" Em stared at her friend in confusion. "The actor? How could you keep that from me?"

Tilly laughed. "No, not the actor. He's the electrician."

"Wow, that shocks me." Last year, he was around a lot, and Em thought she'd have to rewire the entire resort, but come to think of it, only one bill came, and it was to install a new breaker box for the kitchen.

"Shock is a good word. It was quite electrifying."

"What happened?"

"I suppose we lost the spark." She pointed out the window where Miles was standing next to the stack of chairs. "Don't let it happen to you."

"Order up," a cook from behind the line called, and Tilly walked over and placed four plates of quiche and fruit on a tray.

"Since when do we deliver meals to the beach? I thought it was against the rules."

"It is. Why do you ask?"

"Because this is going to Mrs. Blackthorne and family on the beach."

"Who ordered it delivered?"

"Margot, at the request of Miles."

Em set the cups of coffee down. "I'll take care of it and set him straight. He doesn't know any better."

"I'll bring your coffee and their juice."

As Em walked outside, she realized she had no idea who Mrs. Blackthorne was, so she looked around for a family of four. There were five families. It was anyone's guess who was waiting for food. She stared at Miles and gestured with a head nod for him to come over.

He jogged toward her. "Is that for the Blackthornes?"

"It is, but we don't deliver food to the beach."

"Why is that? It seems that a fine establishment like The Brown would cater to their guests' needs."

"We do, but we also look after their safety."

"What could go wrong with a breakfast delivery?" He took the tray. "Follow me."

She turned to see Tilly coming with the drinks. "I got this Tills." Tilly handed her a tray with two cups of coffee and four orange juices before she left.

Miles led her to a family of four who had staked out a claim by the water's edge.

"Good morning, Mrs. Blackthorne. I've got your breakfast," Miles said.

Em stepped forward. "Might I suggest a table inside? We typically don't serve breakfast on the beach."

"Oh," Mrs. Blackthorne said. "We thought breakfast at the beach would be a great way to start the day." She cleared off a towel and patted the space. "Can you imagine anything more delightful?"

Em smiled. "It's just that the birds can be a nuisance."

Mrs. Blackthorne frowned. "In this wind? Look around. There isn't a bird in sight."

Seagulls were nature's laser-guided missiles. Once they locked on to something, they didn't let go, and the destruction they left in their wake was unbelievable.

Miles set the tray on the towel. The four stainless steel cloches caught the sunlight and shined like beacons, and Em knew she'd lost the fight. Maybe some lessons were better off experienced.

"I wish you luck." Em squatted and placed the tray on the towel. She picked up the two coffees and stood. "Enjoy your breakfast."

She moved toward the stack of loungers, counting down from twenty.

Miles took his coffee and asked, "What's going on?"

"You'll see." She handed him his coffee and took a sip. "Twelve, Eleven, Ten."

"What aren't you telling me?"

"I warned you and them, now wait for it." She took another drink. "Six, five." A seagull swooped in and landed on the towel. Seconds later there was another. It was a feeding frenzy with chunks of fruit and egg flying through the air and other birds swooping to grab the airborne pieces.

A scream pierced the air, and Em put her coffee down. "It's time for damage control."

At least two dozen seagulls surrounded the family, pecking at the food. When Mrs. Blackthorne tried to shoo them away, one nipped at her. Within seconds, the family abandoned their perfect place on the beach and ran for The Kessler.

"I'll take care of them. Can you gather the remnants and take the dishes back to the kitchen?"

Miles stared at the melee where another dozen birds had joined to fight over chunks of melon and egg.

He narrowed his eyes. "Did you do this to make The Kessler look bad?"

"I didn't do this. I warned all of you, but you thought you knew better. There are rules for a reason." She could be cruel at times and competitive, but The Kessler belonged to her niece and nephew, and she'd never go out of her way to damage its reputation. "In what world would I want The Kessler to look bad?"

"In a world where Mrs. Blackthorne was the critic."

She laughed. "That woman? No way. She's not sophisticated enough. Besides, she would have known the risks if she were a world traveler. She's no critic."

"I'm pretty sure she'll be critical right now. Why didn't you stop it when you knew what would happen?"

"I tried to tell you both. What was I supposed to do? Refuse to deliver a meal you'd promised them? That would only make you look bad, and that wasn't my objective."

"No, you were teaching me a lesson."

At the time, letting it all happen seemed the thing to do, but now she wasn't sure. She'd made Miles feel bad, and a guest was hurt. "She got bit. When you're done, can you come to look at it?"

She pulled out her phone, called Tilly and asked her to set a table for four, and then walked inside The Kessler. Luckily, the family was in the lobby.

"Mrs. Blackthorne, I've set up a table for you in the dining room of The Brown. Breakfast is on us. We're sorry your experience wasn't perfect, and we'd like to make it up to you."

She held up her bloody finger. "You knew that was going to happen."

Em reached for a Kleenex box and handed it to Mr. Blackthorne, who hadn't said a word since it started. "Apply pressure to the wound."

Em wasn't going to argue with the woman. Telling her she warned her would only put Mrs. Blackthorne on the defensive.

"Follow me, and I'll get you taken care of." She looked over her shoulder and smiled at Margot. "Can you make sure housekeeping gets the Blackthornes' rooms done first? They've had a traumatic experience."

"You got it, boss."

"This way." She led the family to The Brown dining room, where Tilly had prepared a table. In the center was a tray of her famous pastries.

Miles showed up seconds later with a first aid kit.

"I'm so sorry that happened to you. I had no idea the locals were so aggressive." He kneeled before her and took her hand in his. "I'm new here, so please accept my apology." His thumb rubbed Mrs. Blackthorne's palm the whole time, and Em watched as the woman melted in his presence. "Let me see that bite. I'll get it cleaned up and bandaged."

A thread of jealousy moved through her, and she chastised herself for being so immature. She'd asked him to look after the woman and that was exactly what he was doing. "I'm sure it's just a small cut and will heal." It was essential to acknowledge the injury but minimize its damage. She didn't want the Blackthornes leaving and a lawsuit to arrive a week later.

"Better safe than sorry." He let go of Mrs. Blackthorne's hand and opened his first aid kit. "While I clean the wound, Emmaline can get you a new order of quiche and juice."

"I'm over the quiche," Mr. Blackthorne said as he glanced at the menu. "I'll take steak and eggs."

Em wanted to say, *sure you will since I'm buying,* but she didn't. "Absolutely. What about the rest of you?" She glanced at the kids and then Mrs. Blackthorne. The two girls ordered waffles and bacon, and Mrs. Blackthorne ordered the same as her husband. "I'll be right back," she said.

When she got to the kitchen, she told Tilly the order and asked, "Can you help me bury Miles's body after I murder him?"

CHAPTER EIGHTEEN

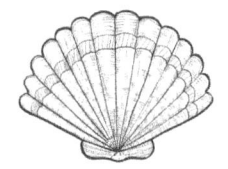

He placed a Band-Aid on Diane Blackthorne's finger. "It's not deep and will heal without a scar." It probably didn't need a bandage but putting one on made her feel better.

"She really should have demanded we eat inside. That woman knew exactly what would happen," Diane said. "She had an evil glint in her eye when those birds were pecking at our breakfast."

He packed up his first aid kit and stood. "I've known Emmaline all my life, and she would have never put you in harm's way." *She might use you as a lesson for me, however.*

"Did you see how she moved out of the way?"

Mr. Blackthorne shook his head. "She did warn us, but you insisted."

"I can assure you," Miles said. "This resort has been in her family since the beginning, and she'd never do anything to jeopardize its reputation."

"There should be signs about the menacing birds."

The girls giggled, and one said, "You screamed like a little girl."

Diane held her bandaged finger in the air. "One nearly amputated my finger."

Mr. Blackthorne took a bite of a pastry. "She warned us."

Emmaline walked out with a tray of orange juice and a pot of coffee. "Your order is in, and I've brought your juice and some of Tilly's famous chicory coffee. I do apologize for the birds. Wildlife can be unpredictable."

"Thankfully, you have a paramedic on staff," Diane said. "That's a smart addition and something you don't find at most hotels."

Emmaline moved next to him. "Miles is quite the find. He's a cowboy by design but a healer at heart."

"Are you married, Miles?"

"No, ma'am."

"Dating?"

"I've got my heart set on someone, but they are as unpredictable as a seagull."

Mrs. Blackthorne laughed. "Let's hope that's where the similarity ends. I'd hate to see you get pecked to death."

"No one is pecking him to death." Emmaline grabbed his first aid kit. "We've got other things to tend to. Say goodbye, and let's go."

As they turned to leave, Mrs. Blackthorne said, "Harold, I think she's his seagull."

When they were out of earshot, Emmaline turned to face him. "Seagull? Really?"

"What? Seagulls are great. They're tenacious and spirited and get what they go after. I'd say you're exactly like a seagull."

"You were flirting with that woman."

"I was not. I was tending to her wound."

She marched toward the boathouse. "It was a scratch.

Did she need all that hand caressing and holding?" She opened the door and walked inside. To the right was a closet that held cleaning supplies. After setting his kit down, she picked up a bucket and filled it with soap and water.

"If she didn't, then she enjoyed the attention, which will go a long way in ensuring she doesn't leave a bad review. In the end, that's all you care about, right? You don't want your precious resort looking bad?" He picked up his kit and walked to the door.

"Where are you going?"

"I've got to put this away and check on Darryl. It's never a good idea to leave a combatant alone. For all I know, he'll find a way to compromise the boathouse, so the next wind takes it down."

"You don't need Daryl for that. It was already near collapse when Carter started working on it." She hefted the bucket of soapy water from the sink. "You're coming back, right?"

He was torn. He's seen a side of Emmaline he wasn't familiar with. A couple of sides. There was the jealous side when she had nothing to be jealous of. Then there was the side of her that wanted to prove a point. Diane was right. She could have refused to serve the meal on the beach, which might have made the Blackthornes unhappy, but it would have avoided the melee that ensued and an injury that could have been much worse. When he first arrived, she'd asked him what qualified him to run a resort, and she was proving that he wasn't qualified at all. Maybe, in the end, he wasn't mad at her. Perhaps he was angry at himself, but he'd need some time alone to think about it.

"I'll see you tomorrow."

"But you promised to help me."

He sighed. "You don't need my help. You've proven that

you've got it all figured out, and I've got a lot to learn. My presence is more of a hindrance than a help."

Before she could respond, he walked out the door. Each step he took made his heart ache. When he entered The Kessler boathouse, he found his brother sitting in a boat drinking a beer.

"Is this how you plan to earn your keep? If so, you might as well pack up and leave." He turned around and walked out. He went straight to the front desk. "Margot, you're in charge. I want you to act like a respectable resort owner. When I get back, everything better still be standing."

"I'm in charge?" Her jaw dropped. "Are you sure that's wise?"

He shrugged. "You couldn't do any worse than I have. I incited a mob of birds to attack a guest. I'd say I'm 0 for 1 today." He pivoted and marched toward the door.

"Where are you going?"

"Out."

"Emmaline won't like that," she said.

"I don't care." He had no idea where Ollie had gone off to after the boathouse, so he whistled and waited. A minute later, his dog trotted forward carrying a sandal that looked very much like the one Emmaline was wearing yesterday. "You can keep that one, buddy." There had to be payback for bad behavior. People said karma always came back to bite them. Well, Emmaline's bite would come in the form of a missing shoe.

Occasionally, he'd judged harshly and acted hastily. Everyone had faults, even Ollie, who had a left foot fetish. His dad and brother were meaner than rabid badgers, and his mother was the caboose on a short line of asshole engines. She went where everyone took her. Emmaline was a lot like his mom. Only she'd rather derail the train than slow down long enough to talk to the engineer. All she had to do was take him aside and explain, and he would have suggested the Blackthornes eat inside as well. But no, she would prove a point at the expense of others.

"Let's go, buddy. I think it's time you met Cricket."

Ollie dropped the sandal and woofed. His tail wagged so quickly that the poor dog had difficulty staying on his feet.

When Miles opened the door to his truck, Ollie jumped inside. When he was behind the steering wheel, he had a perfect view of Emmaline, and she didn't look remorseful for her behavior. She looked pissed because of his.

He put his truck into reverse and pulled out. He had a stop to make on his way. Something about the way Mrs. Blackthorne said that having a paramedic on staff wasn't something a traveler would find at most properties made him think she was more than a family vacationer. If she weren't the critic, then the box of chocolates he planned to pick up at Sweet on You would be a nice gesture. If she was, he hoped it would sweeten her disposition toward both resorts since he'd give them to her from The Kessler and Brown.

He pulled into the parking spot in front of the candy shop and told Ollie to stay. His dog might be able to Houdini himself out of houses, but Miles didn't think he'd be able to get out of a locked vehicle. Before he stepped out, he made sure the windows were down, so Ollie had air.

When he entered the shop, he was greeted by a beautiful brunette. "Welcome to Sweet on You. How can I sweeten your day?"

The display case was full, which meant she was either obsessive about keeping things stocked or the day was slow. And knowing what Cormac told him made him think the latter. He considered Mrs. Blackthorne, and if she'd appreciate the chocolates, then other guests would too.

"I'm Miles, Cormac's uncle."

She cocked her head to the side. "I'm sorry, I don't know who that is."

"He's a younger, better-looking version of me. He comes in here all the time buying candy for his grandma." He didn't know if that's the story Cormac told, but it seemed logical.

"Oh, yeah. Nice guy."

"He really is. You should have pie at Cricket's with him someday. I think you'd both enjoy it."

She smiled. "I've got a daughter."

"That's okay because he's never been known to eat children."

She laughed. "I wasn't implying that. Usually, I pick her up when I get off, and we go home."

"That's fine too. All I'm saying is sometimes what you're looking for is right under your nose."

"Who says I'm looking for something?"

"We're all looking for something." He was looking for the old Emmaline, and though her kisses and lovemaking felt the same, his Emmaline had grown into a woman. She'd had thirty years of hurt and heartbreak to mold her into who she is now. Perhaps he was too hard on her.

"You came in here looking for something. What can I get you?"

He counted the rooms between the two resorts and added a few extras just in case he messed up the tally. When he asked her for dozens of boxes of candies, she lit up like she'd won the lottery, and in a way, she had. He would have never been able to place an order that large without the win. Pay it forward was always his way.

"I'll send Cormac around to pick them up. Can you get them done in an hour?" He figured it would take his nephew that long to get here from the ranch.

She nodded. "They'll be ready."

He paid with his credit card and turned to leave. "I'm heading to Cricket's for pie. It would be nice if you could join Cormac for lunch. You do eat lunch, right?"

"I love lunch."

"Have a good day, Tiffany."

"You know my name."

He smiled. "It's a small town."

Rather than pull out and park a few spaces down, he opened his door and let Ollie out. He wasn't sure if Cricket would allow a dog inside, but it was worth a try. If she didn't, he'd get his meal to go.

He told Ollie to sit when they got to the door. He peeked his head inside and saw Cricket staring at him.

"Miles, is that you? Come and give me some sugar." Cricket rushed forward with her arms opened wide.

Miles smiled. He'd only been to the diner after hours when Cricket had gone home, and one of the high schoolers took over. "I've got a friend with me." He pointed to Ollie. "Can he come in?"

She wrapped him in a hug. "We allow all service dogs to enter." She stepped back, winked, and waved him inside, pointing to a booth under a sign with a chicken holding a *Creative Pork Recipes Cookbook*.

He took a seat, and Ollie crawled under the table.

"What will it be?"

"You choose." He remembered Cricket well enough to know that she'd rather give you what she had than go to a fuss and make you what you want.

"I don't like my men cheap, but I like 'em easy. Blue-plate special for you."

While staying at Marybeth's, he ate a lot of blue-plate specials in the diner. They weren't what he'd call cheap, but they were always delicious.

"Sounds good, Cricket."

"I thought you'd be dining at The Brown, seeing as you and Emmaline are back in the boathouse."

It really was a small town. That was only this morning, and the rumor had hit the wind and traveled far and wide. He imagined it was Tilly or Charlotte or Marybeth who said something. "Those girls can't keep their lips shut."

"It wasn't them. It was Emmaline. She called and said you might be in and asked me to convey her apologies for being, and I quote, 'The painful boil on a monkey's ass.'"

"She said that?"

"Yes, and she asked if you were coming back to please bring her a whole cherry pie and a quart of ice cream." Cricket leaned her hip on the table. "What did you do to my girl?"

His eyes widened. "Me? I didn't do anything. Don't forget, she's the one apologizing."

Cricket leaned in. "She didn't go into details but said something about the day not going quite as planned." She moved in closer. "If things were a little awkward in the boathouse, it's because no one has floated her boat since you left."

He sat back like he'd been slapped. "Impossible."

Cricket crossed her arms and leaned against the booth. "True. That girl is a born-again virgin." She shook her head. "Obviously not after today, but she's never so much as gone on a real date." She lifted her hand and wagged a finger. "I suppose that's a tiny lie. There was that one guy, but he only made it to the booth across from her, and I kicked him out. He'd been sitting in the same booth with Charlotte the night before. My girls deserve better than that."

"She didn't look sorry when I left. She looked like she was ready to skin me alive."

"Emmaline never does anything with subtlety. That girl does everything with bravado. I'd bet she didn't think you'd leave her again, but you did."

His heart lurched. "I didn't leave her. I left her to come and eat."

"Did she know that?"

"Yes, because she called you with a to-go order."

"That was her being hopeful." She pushed off the booth. "I'll get that order ready."

He sat there and thought about what Cricket had said, and he felt lower than an ant in a ditch. Emmaline's biggest fear was that he'd leave again, and his was that she'd push him away. They were both doing their best to sabotage what they had together.

"Cricket?" He called from his booth. "Can I get that to go?"

She tapped her head. "I already put the order in that way. I'll get the pie and ice cream ready too."

He shook his head. "She won't need it."

"That's my boy. You were always my favorite."

CHAPTER NINETEEN

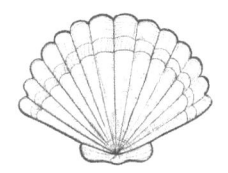

"And he left me," Em said as she poured herself a cup of coffee and sat at her kitchen table talking to Charlotte and Marybeth on a three-way call. Had it only been a day since she sat there getting all gussied up to make Miles regret leaving her? This was history repeating itself, only she was squarely at fault this time. Why she did what she did, she couldn't say, but she imagined it was to prove something. She'd been proving herself worthy all her life, and then Miles comes along and changes everything.

"He didn't leave you. He's probably just taking a break. You know, sometimes when you call and I don't answer, I'm here, but I need a break too," Marybeth said. "You can be intense."

"What?" She didn't usually take anything in her coffee, but today she put three teaspoons of sugar because her sweet meter was falling below empty. "You ignore my calls? At least Charlotte doesn't abandon me. Right Charlotte?"

Her friend took far too long to answer. "I try not to. I was there yesterday when you needed a makeover."

Marybeth cleared her throat. "Don't you leave me

hanging out to dry. You were home that weekend she wanted us to come over and watch movies, but you told her you had plans in Austin."

"Oh my God. You lied about that?" She sat alone, watched *The Notebook* by herself, and bawled ugly tears for an hour.

"Well," Charlotte said in a pitch that would make a dog squeal. "It wasn't a real big lie. I watched Austin Powers with Tilly. I couldn't do *The Notebook* one more time. Honey, we've watched it so many times that you know the script."

Em gasped. "Tilly said she was checking out a new farmer's market in Beaumont and wouldn't be back to town in time for movie night. She had all kinds of fruits and veggies when she showed up the next day." There was no way her closest friend of all would betray her. It couldn't be true.

"She stopped at Kroger on the way to work that morning," Charlotte said.

"I can't believe it. What kind of friends are you?"

"The kind who love you but know when they've hit their capacity. We've been filling your emptiness for years. And we don't mind, but sometimes we need to fill our tanks too," Marybeth said.

"And Austin Powers does it for you? I thought you had better taste. At least when Tilly abandons me by herself, it's for David Hasselhoff."

"Wait," Marybeth said. "The actor?"

"No, the electrician, but what does it matter? You lie to me." Her mind moved through a dozen dates where all her friends were mysteriously absent or busy. "You act like I'm high maintenance. I don't ask for much. All I wanted was your time."

"Don't be mad, Em," Charlotte said. "Now tell us what happened with Miles. Tilly said you were in the boathouse for hours. Did it really take that long?"

Em wanted to be furious with her friends and hang up, but she needed them right this minute, so she would postpone her rage and hang up on them later.

"No, we were cleaning the cobwebs out."

Charlotte sucked in a breath. "Oh honey, I know it's been a lifetime, but cobwebs? Is that even possible?" She made a *tsk tsk* sound. "Marybeth, I told you we should have left a tube of lube. She's like a rusty gate that needs some WD-40. A little dab would do a body good."

"Not my hoo-haw. We were cleaning out the cobwebs from the boathouse. Don't forget, there's a critic either here or coming into town, and I want to be prepared."

"See, you need a program," Charlotte said. "I don't know how many steps it will take to get you off the resort sauce, but you have a man you've been in love with all your life. You're alone in the boathouse, and all you did was clean cobwebs? Your priorities are skewed. One day you'll be lying on your deathbed with Marybeth praying over you, and I guarantee you won't wish you'd impressed a stupid critic. You'll be looking at your old, wrinkled hands, wondering why someone isn't holding them, and telling you everything will be okay."

"Harsh," Em said.

"Sometimes the truth is brutal," Marybeth said. "Now tell us what you did to make Miles mad."

"Why do you think it's my fault?" They were both silent, and she could see their expressions in her mind. Charlotte would be halfway through an eye roll, and Marybeth would have that constipated look she got when she'd lost her patience. "Okay, it's my fault." She told them what happened, and they agreed that she could have handled it differently.

"Now what?" Marybeth asked.

"I'm waiting for a cherry pie and a quart of ice cream."

"I can't make it, honey. I have a hair appointment," Charlotte said.

"You don't have to lie to me. I'm not asking you to bring me anything."

After an exasperated sigh, Charlotte said, "I truly have a hair appointment. You saw my hair yesterday. It looked like someone hid a quiche in it, and the seagulls went to work. Dolly has her job cut out for her."

"I can pick up pie if you'd like, honey. Raleigh can wait for his dinner."

Em looked at the clock hanging on the wall. It always made her smile with its bright yellow sunflower petals marking the hour, a ladybug marking the minutes, and the stem clicking back and forth to keep track of the seconds. But today, she frowned because it was just after lunchtime, and Marybeth was talking about dinner, which meant she'd had her fill of Em. "I asked Cricket to send it home with Miles if he showed up."

"And if he doesn't?"

"Don't forget, I've got a world-class baker in the kitchen."

"You okay?" Charlotte asked.

"Yeah. I'll be fine. I'm always okay."

"Are we okay?" Marybeth asked.

"I want to be mad at you, but I can't. I know you're not trying to lick the red off my candy; somewhere in all this is a message. I'll figure it out while I eat my pie."

"Love you, sugar," Charlotte said.

"I'll pray for you," Marybeth added.

Em chuckled. "I'll skip tonight's episode of *How to Get Away with Murder* to keep you both safe."

They hung up, and she sat there and sipped her too-sweet coffee, wondering where Miles was and if he was bringing the pie.

As the moments passed, she considered all that had happened that day. They were doing what they did thirty years ago. They weren't communicating. The only difference now was she was mature enough to know she had to listen more than she spoke. It was all good in theory, but now to put it into action.

A knock sounded at her door, and her heart leaped. It was either Miles, or the girls had called Tilly.

She put her cup in the sink and went to the door. Before she opened it, she pinched her cheeks and finger-combed her hair just in case. She may have felt low, but that was no excuse to look like something the sea churned up from the bottom and spit out in a storm.

At the second knock, she opened the door to find Miles standing there. He had a to-go bag in his hand but no pie and no quart of vanilla. Ollie stood next to him, holding a sandal.

"Were they out of pie?"

"Can we come in?"

She stepped aside so Miles and the dog could enter, then leaned down to pet Ollie. She recognized the jewels bedazzling the shoe in his mouth. "Is that my sandal?"

Ollie dropped it at her feet.

"He's sorry."

She picked up the slobbery shoe and shook her head. "I guess we like what we like."

"I love you, Emmaline, and I'm sorry too. I should have learned from the past. I should have stayed and talked.

Thirty years ago, I left because that's what everyone expected, but I regret not fighting for us."

"Did you say you loved me?" How long had it been since she'd heard those words? She hadn't realized how love-starved she was until that moment.

"I did say it, and I always will. I also said I'm sorry."

"I love you too." She tugged him into the entryway and shut the door. "And I'm also sorry. I shouldn't have expected you to know, and when you thought it was a good idea, I could have explained rather than let you experience the lesson. I feel awful. You left, and I felt so lonely."

"What now?" he asked.

"Do you forgive me?"

"I'll always forgive you. But what about me? Will you forgive me?"

She lifted on tiptoes and pressed her lips to his. "There's nothing to forgive." Ollie whined, and she shook her head at him. "I don't know how you got my sandal, but I forgive you too." She looked down at the bag. "What did you bring?"

"Dinner."

"What happened to my pie and ice cream?"

"Baby, you don't need that. Whatever you need, I'm here to give it to you."

"But what if I wanted dessert?"

He grinned. "They say life's uncertain. Eat dessert first. I have lots of sweet kisses to offer among other things" He placed the bag on the entry table. "Would you care to show me your room?"

CHAPTER TWENTY

Miles was in the kitchen an hour later, looking at his meatloaf, mashed potatoes, and peas. "How long should I heat this?" he called to Emmaline upstairs.

"Try three minutes," she answered back. "Have you seen my shoe?"

Since she said shoe, as in singular, he didn't need to see it to know where it was. "Ollie?" His dog slinked around the corner carrying a leather loafer. "You're a naughty boy," he said and took the shoe from the dog's mouth. "It's down here."

"How in the world?" Emmaline trotted down the stairs wearing one shoe and bounced into the kitchen. He'd never seen her so happy. "Are you going to share?" She removed the food from the to-go container and put it on a plate.

"I'll share everything with you." He dried off her shoe and set it on the floor so she could slip her foot inside. It wasn't a glass slipper, but he felt like this was the stuff fairytales were made of. He'd left his kingdom years ago, and life led him back to the only woman he'd ever loved—his Cinderella. Today's relationship mishap made him realize that he never wanted anything like a misunderstanding to come between them again. "Can we make a pact?"

"Yes, unless you want to seal it with blood. I did that with the girls in junior high and got an infection. My index finger swelled twice its size, and I had to get an IV antibiotic drip to get rid of it." Ollie nudged at her foot. She looked down at him. "Thanks for taking care of my shoe." She put the dish in the microwave and set the timer for three minutes. "Do you think he needs therapy?"

"He's the canine version of Imelda Marcos, the Philippine dictator's wife who had over a thousand pairs of shoes. All he wants is shoes."

"What he probably needs is a leash. How did he sneak up there and steal my shoe without us knowing?"

Miles smiled and kissed her lips. "We were busy."

"Yes, we were." The microwave dinged, and she pulled the meal from it and set it on the table. "What now?"

"What do you mean?"

"I mean, where do we go from here?" She grabbed two forks and sat at the table. Cricket's meals were over-the-top big and could feed both of them easily.

"I like here just fine. Why do we have to decide about tomorrow when we should thoroughly enjoy today?"

She nodded. "You're right."

Someone knocked at her door, and Ollie woofed and ran for it. It wasn't that he wanted to see who was there. He was more interested in the shoes they were wearing. Nirvana, for him, was anytime they visited a house where people had to remove their shoes before entering. He'd be sadly disappointed at Emmaline's liberal shoe policy.

"It's probably Tilly checking on me. I wasn't in a good place earlier." She rose from her chair and walked toward the door.

"I know," he called after her. "You wanted a whole pie and a tub of ice cream."

She grabbed the door handle, and before she opened the door, she looked over her shoulder. "But I got you instead."

"I hope that's better than ice cream."

"Best dessert ever."

She opened the door, and from his spot at the table, he saw Cormac. He'd forgotten about the candy.

"Hey, Cormac," Emmaline said. "What brings you here?"

He lifted two large bags. "Special delivery for Uncle Miles."

"Come in. we were just sitting down to eat your uncle's meatloaf. There's plenty for everyone."

Cormac touched his belly. "I'm as full as a tick." He walked inside and looked around. Miles followed his line of sight to the garden-like atmosphere of Emmaline's house. He hadn't noticed anything but her when he entered earlier, but now that he was more focused, he saw that she'd decorated it like a secret garden. He'd only been in the house a few times before, and it never looked bright and happy. It had been dark wood and pipe tobacco. A heaviness hovered like smoke in the residence, so they never hung out at Emmaline's home.

"Wow, this place is—"

"I know, it's over the top, but when everyone died, I needed something light and airy." She returned to the table, and Cormac followed with the bags. "The house was depressing with its darkness."

"It's amazing," Miles said. "I love how you brought the outdoors inside. Even on a rainy day, it's sunny in here." That was the exact color of the walls, sunshine yellow.

Cormac took a seat. "Did you ask Tiffany on a date?"

Emmaline snapped her attention to him. "Not for me."

Cormac's cheeks turned cherry pie red. "I meant, did you tell her I wanted to date her?"

All eyes were on him. Emmaline dug into the mashed potatoes and gravy and watched him like he was a new episode of her favorite soap opera.

"No, I just told her you were a nice person, and I thought you'd enjoy each other's company."

"She asked me to lunch." A big grin nearly split his nephew's face.

"Did you say yes?"

He nodded. "That's why I'm so full."

"Did you pick up the bill?"

Emmaline sat up. "That's tricky these days."

Cormac whistled. "I'm telling you. You think you're doing the right thing by offering to pay, and some girls get all mad because they think you're insinuating that they can't pay for themselves, or they'll owe you something. I want to pay for my date because I asked her to come and eat with me."

"But she asked you," Emmaline said. "So, how did you handle it?"

He smiled. "I told her it would be an honor to buy her lunch, and she let me." Miles lifted his hand for a high five, and Cormac smacked it mid-air. "Then she told me I was sweet and gave me a box of chocolates." He pointed to the bags. "Not the chocolates you ordered for the guests but a box she put together for me, and it had a heart candy right in the middle of the box. Do you think that means something?"

They both looked at Emmaline because they were dudes and had no idea how women thought.

"I wouldn't propose tomorrow, but I think it means she might be sweet on you."

Cormac blushed. "I hope you're right. I've been admiring that woman from afar for at least a year."

"A year?" Emmaline asked. "Why haven't you made a move?"

Cormac seemed to fold in on himself. "I don't have much to offer a person. Who wants to date a poor man when they could have a rich man? Don't forget, she was married to the guy who owns that building."

Emmaline seemed to bristle before them. "Travis Townsend had nothing but money to offer and look what it got him—a divorce." She passed the plate to Miles, who hadn't eaten much of it. "Besides, money isn't everything." She pointed to Miles. "I love your uncle, and he probably doesn't have two nickels to rub together."

Miles wanted to laugh. Eventually, he'd have to tell her the truth. "I've got a few nickels saved up."

Cormac pointed to the bags. "Those cost a pretty penny, and Tiffany said to say thanks. Because of your order, she can pay the rent this month on the shop."

"How much candy did you buy and why? We never put candy in the rooms."

"I know I should have consulted you first, but after Diane got nipped because of me, I thought it might be a nice gesture, and if it was a nice gesture for her, then it was probably a nice move for all the guests in both resorts."

"You bought boxes of chocolates for all the guests? Including those staying at The Brown?"

He shrugged. "I didn't want you to think I was competing with you. If you don't think it's a good idea, then fine, but I think it could be that little extra that makes a difference. These aren't just any chocolates. They're custom confections from Sweet On You. It's a win-win for Tiffany and us."

"They couldn't have been cheap. I'll pay you back for the purchase." She rose and pulled a checkbook from a nearby drawer. "How much do I owe you?"

"Nothing. I got it."

"Miles, you don't have a job."

"I do have a job and a place to live. Carter and Brie are paying me well for taking care of things."

"He has to have some money. He came here looking to buy the place." Cormac laughed. "Silly Uncle Miles didn't realize it would be in the millions."

He sat back and let his nephew laugh at his expense. Ultimately, the laugh would be on them because he could buy two Kessler resorts and still have money left over. He'd looked up its value and found it estimated at around eight million if it was in pristine condition, which it wasn't.

Emmaline took his hand. "I love that you thought you could."

"Anything is possible if your heart is in it."

"I'd like to help with the candy," she said.

He decided to use Cormac's line. "I'd be honored if you'd let me pay."

She giggled. "You win."

"Speaking of honored … Grandma would like you both to come to the ranch tonight for dinner if you can get away. She's making your favorite cornbread casserole, southern fried chicken, and collard greens."

"She invited me too?" Emmaline asked.

"Yes, she specifically said to include you." He rose from his chair. "Do you know where I can find my dad?"

"Last time I looked, he was drinking a beer in The Kessler boathouse."

"Do you mind if I go inside there to check it out?" Cormac walked toward the door.

"Have at it."

"Can I tell Grams to expect you?"

Emmaline nodded. "We'll be there."

Cormac left, and Miles looked at Emmaline when she returned from the door. "That was easy."

"Contrary to rumors, I'm not always difficult to deal with. Your mother is sick, and if she wants us to come to dinner nightly, then we'll be there."

"We will?"

"Remember your rule?"

"What rule is that?"

"Let's take it one day at a time. Well, today is the only day you may get. Who knows how long your mother has. My sister was here one day and gone the next. I never even got to say goodbye. Don't let a second pass that you might regret."

He rose and rushed to her, pulling her into his arms and kissing her like it might be his last chance because she was right. No one knew when it might be. "I love you, Emmaline Brown. Thirty years might have passed, but it feels like yesterday you were planning our wedding."

Her breath caught, and he worried that he might have brought up an unpleasant memory. "I'm sorry."

She gave him a curious look. "Why are you sorry? I messed up too."

He liked the mature Emmaline, who was willing to take responsibility for her part in their demise. "We can spend the rest of our moments making it up to each other."

"I like that idea better."

"Speaking of moments, not that it matters, but has there been anyone since me? Cricket alluded to the fact that you might have never ... you know ... since we ..." He cocked his head and nodded to the stairs that led to her bedroom.

"Cricket what?" She huffed. "I can't believe she told you that. What exactly did she say?"

He grimaced. He didn't want to cause a rift between the two women, but he knew he had to tell Emmaline, or she'd go to the diner and get it straight from Cricket's mouth. "She said, and I quote, 'That girl is a born-again virgin.'"

"I'm going to kill her."

"I think she was trying to make me feel special."

"Do you feel special?"

"Of course, you always make me feel that way, but is it true?"

She cleared off the table and walked toward the door. "This is another example of how a woman can do things herself. You know a woman doesn't need a man to orgasm, right? I'm happy to discuss my sex life with you, but if you want a full accounting of what I've been up to for the last thirty years, I'll expect the same. Shall we have a seat and exchange names, or would you rather help me put fresh wood by the fire pit?"

He rushed around her to open the door. "Where do I get the wood?"

CHAPTER TWENTY-ONE

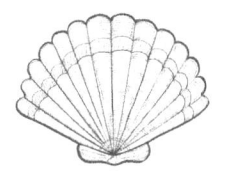

There were some things Em didn't discuss with anyone, and her frequency of lovers was one of them. It wasn't as if the opportunities didn't present themselves. There were always men looking for love, but her heart was damaged, and she never felt right about promoting a faulty product to someone. Though the hurts were still there, they were no longer embedded deep inside. They were at the surface and healing because Miles had returned.

Whoever said you could never go back was wrong. Sometimes it was necessary to go back to move forward. Miles had been an excruciating part of her past, but he was also becoming an exciting part of her future.

"Do you set the fire pit up every day?" Miles stacked tinder and wood in the stone-circled pit. "I don't remember this being here when we were kids."

She shook her head. "It wasn't. Dad didn't want an open fire on the property." He never gave people much credit and worried they'd burn down everything he'd built. "I put just enough wood so they can build a decent fire, make some s'mores, and tell a good story or two." She pointed to the bucket of water. "It's clear in the brochure that when they are finished, they have to douse the embers with water."

"I rarely agreed with your father about anything, but unsupervised fires can be problematic."

"People are often smarter than they look."

"I'm not talking about how smart people look. I've seen some brilliant people do some stupid things. I'm just surprised you'll control everything from the seagulls to the chewed gum on the bottoms of the tables, but you'll let guests start fires at will."

She hadn't thought of it in those words, but he had a point. Then again, she couldn't control everything. She tried to for years, and then her parents passed. A new normal began, and she breathed a little easier because she wasn't reminded of their daily disappointment. Her sister was easier to work for, but she was in control. It wasn't until her brother-in-law and her sister passed that she could make decisions regarding the resort; the fire pit was the first she'd made. As a kid, it was the one thing she always wanted. It was a place where families could gather, and tell stories while they roasted marshmallows. That was always her dream. She wanted those family moments, and those stories, but all she got were rules and condemnation. When the handyman made a circle with boulders, all she heard was her father's voice tell her it was irresponsible, and she'd burn the place down, but it had been years, and nothing devastating had happened. She never got the warm fuzzy experience, but she gave it to others.

"I think my father punished me because of you."

Miles stopped stacking the wood and looked at her. "Because of the deal?"

She shrugged. "It was just another thing that made him believe I was bad at decision-making."

Miles frowned, and she watched the light die in his eyes.

"It's amazing how one decision changed the lives of so many." He walked to her and wrapped her in his arms, hugging her tightly.

There was no question—the best place to be was wrapped in one of his hugs. She knew it back then and knew it now. Only back then, she was too young to have a voice. Or, after so many years of being silenced, she was programmed not to use her voice. She had a reputation as being the wild Brown girl—the unpredictable child of Bessy and Horace. In hindsight, her unpredictability was all she could control. The problem with the heir and the spare mentality was the spare's only purpose was to step in when the heir could no longer perform their duty, but the spare was reminded constantly that they were not the chosen.

She let the warmth of his embrace soak into her core before she stepped back. "It's in the past. and we need to let it go." It was okay to revisit the past to get perspective, but she didn't want to live there. How many years had been wasted because the one time she needed to be unpredictable, she wasn't? The one time when Miles needed her rebellious side to rule, and she had buried it.

She followed his line of sight toward The Kessler boathouse. Darryl and Cormac were talking near the dock.

"It's hard to let go when the present keeps hitting you over the head with the past."

She smiled. When it came to getting good advice, she never went to her mother. She always went to Cricket because somehow, Cricket seemed to understand her.

"A wise older woman once told me that the universe works in mysterious ways. Sometimes you need to stop and listen to its message. If you refuse, she'll chuck a pebble at your head. If you still refuse, she'll use a rock. Then a brick, and then a boulder." She nodded toward Darryl. "We've made up, so maybe it's time to make things straight with your brother. If you can't see eye-to-eye on everything, then maybe just see that your mother is happy for the days she has left."

"I know you're right. The universe doesn't have to hit Darryl upside the head with a brick. I can do it for her later."

She sighed and thought back to the tragic loss of her sister. "I wish I had one more day to spend with Olivia. We weren't all that close because I was jealous of her. She had it all. The funny thing is that now that I can see clearly, she had nothing. She was in love with a man she couldn't have." Saying it out loud made her realize she'd suffered the same fate. Only Miles wasn't married to another. "She was in a loveless marriage. The only good thing that came out of it was Brie."

"Do you regret not having children?"

She tilted her head back and forth. "I don't think I would have been a great mother."

"Not true. You would have been an excellent mother."

She laughed. "Nope, just look at what I did to get Brie back to Willow Bay. I told her I had the big C."

He moved to the pit and placed the last piece of wood on the stack. "But your intentions were good."

She took his hand and led him toward the water. It was a beautiful day, the wind had died down, but the water was still rough. It licked at the shore, leaving buried treasures of sand, seaweed, and driftwood.

"Brie wasn't living. She was attached to a house and its memories. That's no life."

He stood back and stared at her. He didn't have to say

the words because the message was in his eyes. She was guilty of the same.

"This is different. It's a job. It supports me and many in the community."

"Okay, if that's the story you tell yourself. Would you ever leave it?"

"For what?"

They made it to the beach and stood there staring at the waves as they crashed and retreated.

"Me. What if I asked you to leave with me again?"

It was as if he'd punched her in the gut. From his voice and expression, this didn't seem to be a theoretical question. It seemed like he was asking for real. "And do what? My life is here."

He took her hand, and they walked down the beach. "Is it?"

"Yes, and so is yours. You came here to run The Kessler."

He shook his head. "No, I came here to reconcile the past. I missed an opportunity to make things right with my father, and I won't pass it up with my mother." He looked over his shoulder toward The Kessler boathouse. "The jury is still out with my brother. Right now, I'm trying to offer him what he refused me: kindness, patience, and compassion. But that brick is looking better and better by the minute."

Miles had remained the same in many ways, but the older version of him was more patient and kinder, whereas the older version of her was the opposite. "What made you so—"

"Handsome?" he said jokingly.

"No, I was going to say—"

"Easygoing?"

She laughed. "That wouldn't have been the word I chose, but I suppose it works."

"I've seen a lot of death in my years, and not one person has looked at me and said that they wished they had lived a life filled with more hate and anger before they passed. I've held the hands of children and the elderly as they took their last breath; all they wanted was more time. I could say I wasted the last thirty years, but if I'm honest, maybe I needed those years to teach me to appreciate every second I'm here."

"Are you staying?" She held her breath and waited for him to answer.

"Where would I go?"

She picked up a stick and drew a heart in the sand. "I want you to stay because you want to, not because you don't have choices."

"I have choices, Emmaline. I'm not the penniless cowboy who left you. I've got money."

He'd always been a prideful man. She didn't know how much a paramedic made, but she imagined it hadn't made him rich. As she thought about the property that she co-owned with Brie, she wasn't rich either. She was, but it was all in the land, not her bank account. She never wanted for anything, but her needs were pretty simple. Or they had been until Miles came back. Now she needed him like her next breath.

She twirled in a circle with her arms spread wide. "This is almost like we envisioned." They turned and walked back toward the house, and she saw that the heart she'd drawn near the shore had washed away.

He squeezed her hand. "Almost, but we didn't build this together."

"But we can build it into something more."

He looked around. "I think it's all it can be. I'd still love a chance to build something with you. Something that's ours. Isn't it time we stopped living up to the expectations of others and started pleasing ourselves?"

She wrapped her hands around his arm and leaned her head on his shoulder. "And leave all this? No way. We don't need to reinvent the wheel. All we need to do is keep this one turning. Say you'll stay with me."

He didn't hesitate. "You are my future, and while I would have loved to start where we left off, anywhere you are is where I want to be."

She glanced at her watch. "Right now, I need to be at the front desk. Don't you have painting to do? Brie and Carter will be back soon, and it would be great if they could come home to something different, something fresh and new."

"Fresh and new sounds good."

She kissed him, and they separated on the path to the parking lot. She took the steps into The Brown two at a time. She was feeling lighter and heavier at the same time. Miles was here, which made her happy, but despite what he had just said about Em being his future, he didn't seem as committed to the resort as she was, but then again, he hadn't been raised to run it.

CHAPTER TWENTY-TWO

Miles got Cormac to help him finish the living room, and they moved on to the hallway and kitchen.

"Do you ever do anything with your dad?"

Cormac laughed as he did the detailed cutting in where the wall and ceiling met. When Miles turned fifty, the first thing to go was his eyesight, so leaving the straight lines to Cormac seemed prudent.

"With him? You mean like this, where we chat and share stories?" He shook his head. "Nope. I do what I'm told. I work for him more than anything else."

Miles felt terrible for the kid, who wasn't a kid but a grown man. "I understand." He could play this in two ways. He could bad mouth his brother, which would be so easy, or he could point out that his father didn't know any better. "It's easier to do what you know, and all Darryl knows is how to do what we taught him. Grandpa wasn't one to chitchat. He was a man who said jump, and the only acceptable response was to ask how high."

"Grandpa was the worst." He dipped his brush into the milky white paint and slicked at the edge between the wall and ceiling, creating a perfectly ruler-straight line. "He was just plain old mean."

"I think he had a tough life. Ranching isn't easy, and it's not cheap. You'd think letting a bunch of cows roam the land eating and mating would be simple and inexpensive, but everything needs care. When droughts hit, and we've seen a few, he had to supplement with hay and feed. There are vet costs, transportation of the cattle to market, and all that."

"Did he really lie on the forms about the pedigree of the cattle?"

He didn't want to stir up dung, but the truth was usually better in the end. "He did, but over the years, I see why. I think he lied to make things easier on the rest of us." When he left, his family was pretty well-off. Some would call them filthy rich, but he never saw that part. What his father and mother had, they'd worked for. Their rule was that the harder you worked, the luckier you got. His father truly wanted to pass on something bigger than he'd received when Miles's grandfather died and left him the ranch.

"It backfired because, as my father pointed out, they got sued and lost everything." Cormac stopped and looked at Miles. "I don't blame you for my lot in life. If Grandpa was cheating people, then he got what he deserved. My only regret is that I've stuck around out of family loyalty, and I don't have a pot to piss in or a window to throw it out of. If I had more, I could help Tiffany."

Miles knew how that felt. If he'd had more, Emmaline might have left with him. He was so angry and bitter for years, but looking back, it would have been tragic to drag her away from her life with nothing to offer.

"How was the lunch date with Tiffany?"

"It was great. She has a little girl named Ava who I'd

like to meet in person. I've seen them in town, and she's as cute as a button." He laughed. "Now I sound like Grandma."

Miles looked at his phone. "Speaking of Grandma, we'd better get going. She doesn't like people disrespecting her time. Or she didn't use to."

"Still doesn't. That will get you a severe ear-pulling." He pointed to his right lobe. "I swear this one is longer than the left."

"Since I like my ears the way they are, let's clean up and get over to the ranch." He wanted to ask if Darryl was coming but didn't want to ruin his day with thoughts of having to share dinner with the crotchety old cuss. He chuckled at the thought of Darryl being old since he was only two years older than Miles.

Once the brushes and rollers were cleaned, Cormac left him to shower and get Emmaline.

EMMALINE SAT beside him in his truck—not on her side next to the door but right beside him like they had in the old days. She wore a sweet pink sundress that skimmed the top of her knees and the bejeweled sandals that Ollie loved so much. His heart beat so fast that he had to slow it down with calm, even breaths.

"I always loved your mother's cornbread casserole," she said. "It's like magic in a pan."

"I think it's the cast-iron skillet. The thing hasn't been washed in a hundred years. That pan was my grandma's and hers before that. Mom wipes it out and slathers more oil on it."

She shuddered beside him. "I don't want to think about it, but I want to gobble an entire pan of it up."

"I'll fight you for the last piece."

She leaned against him. "Haven't we fought enough? Let's make love, not war."

"Shall I take you home and upstairs to your wonderfully soft bed?" He gripped the steering wheel, trying to control all the feelings welling up inside him—the first being desire. The second was a sense of nostalgia that raced through him like one too many brandies on a winter's night, making him feel love drunk.

"And miss the cornbread casserole?"

He let go of the wheel with one hand and took her hand in his. "I can't believe my lovemaking comes in second to food."

She turned, and he caught a glimpse of her smile. "I need the food to keep up with your lovemaking."

They wound their way to the ranch, and while it seemed inland, there was a thin strip of land that met a craggy cliff. He and Emmaline used to sit at the edge and watch the sunset.

"Does it feel weird to enter the ranch after all these years?" she asked.

"It takes me back a time. When I drove here the last time, I was shocked to see how run-down it had all become. The land is overgrown because there are no cattle to speak of. Darryl has a few heads but nothing that would tame the land."

They turned into the drive and moved under the McClintock Ranch sign. It was old and worn, with the wood cracking and peeling.

"Why doesn't he mow it down? It's a fire hazard growing this tall."

Miles pointed to the large mower off to the side of the road. One tire was bent at an odd angle. "Looks like he didn't maintain the machinery." In truth, it didn't look like his brother had done much since their father died five years ago.

"It's a shame because this land has so much to offer."

He smiled at all the memories. Mostly sad, but there were a few that would stay with him forever, like the first time he made love to Emmaline on a blanket at the cliff's edge. His family's land held some of his worst memories, but it also had the absolute best.

"I think it would make an amazing dude ranch."

"What do you think will happen to it after your mother passes?"

He'd been thinking about that, but Emmaline halted his dreams of owning a ranch when she said she wouldn't leave the resort.

"I imagine Darryl will sell it." Hopefully, he'll take care of Cormac, but Miles imagined his brother had the same philosophy as his father. Anything Cormac had, he'd have to earn until Darryl's death, and then he'd get whatever was left. Knowing Darryl, it wouldn't be much. Maybe he'd buy it for Cormac and set his nephew up to have something more than unfulfilled dreams and regrets.

As they approached the house, he heard Emmaline gasp. "My goodness. It's so much older than I remembered. Has no one done anything in thirty years?"

This is where his guilt came in. Because he'd uncovered the truth, everyone and everything suffered.

"I caused this." He parked the truck next to a car he didn't recognize and stared at the shutter hanging off-balance from the window. He took in the once-blue paint that had faded to gray.

She cupped the side of his face and made him turn toward her. "No. They did this. It's not your fault." She tilted her head and smiled. "I've had time to think about all of this. I'd rather marry an honest man than a rich man. Integrity is a form of wealth that many people will never acquire."

He kissed her before he exited the truck, wondering, *what if I could give you both?*

He opened her door and helped her out just as the front door opened and a suited man exited.

"Thanks, May. I'll update your documents and put them into the permanent file."

"Thank you, Travis. I appreciate you getting here so soon. As you know, I don't have a lot of time."

Miles's heart felt like someone had stabbed him, reached into the hole, and pulled on his aorta. Looking at his mother, she seemed to have aged another ten years in the day since he saw her.

"Travis Jackson, is that you?"

The man nodded. "Hey, Miles. It's good to see you back." He looked at Emmaline. "Hello, Em. It's been a while."

Miles didn't want to read into anything, but they seemed to be familiar.

"Travis, why don't you come by the resort soon? There are some changes I need to make to my will."

Miles breathed easier, knowing that the familiarity might be because they'd done business.

"I'll call you next week." Travis walked down the steps, got in his sedan, and drove away.

"Should I be worried?"

She laughed. "Nope. He's a bad kisser." She left him on the gravel and moved toward his mother. "May, you look exhausted. Let me take over while you and Miles visit."

"Wait, you kissed him?" He walked inside the house, closed the door behind him, and followed Emmaline and his mother into the kitchen. It was a large ranch kitchen with a table that sat a good twenty people. Not small people but large ranch hands who used to show up for their three meals daily in this kitchen. May had set the table at one end with five places. Yep, Darryl and Cormac were coming.

"We aren't talking about that, remember?"

He knew she was right. Talking about past relationships never went well for the present love, so he let it go.

Emmaline pulled out the chair at the end of the long table and helped his mother into her seat. It was odd to see her sitting there as he'd only seen his grandfather and father there. He imagined Darryl sat there when he was present. Wouldn't he be surprised to find Emmaline had demoted his position? Then again, his mother had done that when she fired him the other day.

"I'll check the food while you two spend a moment together." Emmaline moved to the old six-burner stove where pots sat on top billowing steam, and the oven light gave them a peek at the old cast-iron skillet with its golden cornbread inside.

He lifted his nose into the air and breathed in his past. Memories of days gone filled his mind. He saw a table with hungry men who entertained him with stories of roping, branding, and cattle raids. He imagined half of the hands were wanted in some county for thieving, but they were hard-working, salt-of-the-earth types who had filled his world with dreams of a different future.

The front door opened, and Darryl walked inside. "What was Travis doing here?" He stared at his mother, who sat at the head of the table. Watching Darryl enter the kitchen was like watching a woman walk into the men's bathroom. They usually stared for a few minutes before they turned and hightailed it out of there. Darryl had that out-of-place look about him, but there was nowhere to turn and run.

"I had some final will business left to take care of."

Darryl narrowed his eyes. "You put him back in it. After all I've done for the last thirty years?"

May pointed to the spaces on the sides of the table and told them to each take a seat. She turned to Emmaline. "Dinner's ready. Can you dish it up while I explain the what's what to my hard-headed sons?"

"Sure thing, May. What about Cormac?"

"Oh, he'll be here in a minute. He doesn't like what happens when he's late."

Miles laughed because he knew what happened, and a minute later, the sound of Cormac's boots thunked down the stairs, and he ran through the hall to the kitchen with his hair still dripping wet.

"Did I miss anything?"

Miles glanced around the room at Emmaline plating their dinner and Darryl looking like he already wanted to throw up.

"No, I'd say you're right on time." May pointed to the chair next to Darryl. "Have a seat."

Emmaline placed a plate of steaming hot food in front of everyone and took the seat beside Miles

May lowered her head and said, "Bless this food and all that have none. Amen."

They all followed with an "Amen," but no one took a bite until May did. It was like she was the queen; no one ate until she did, and they would be finished when she was.

She took a nibble and raised her hand. "I'm going to say a few things, and then I'm heading to bed. I expect the food to get eaten and the kitchen cleaned."

"I don't clean kitchens," Darryl said.

"You do tonight," May said. Though her voice was weak, the message was strong. She had things to say and didn't want to waste time. "Travis Jackson was here to change my will. As you know, I'm dying. With the rate things are going, it will come quickly. Thankfully, I'm not in any pain. That seems to be the way with some lung cancers. They don't call it the silent killer for nothing." She took in several wheezy breaths and continued. "What I have to say is the law. Anyone who argues will get themselves written out of the will. Do you understand?"

They all nodded except for Darryl, whose face was redder than a freshly-fired branding iron.

"This property has been in the family since Abel McClintock homesteaded it in the early 1800s. The only wish your father left behind was that it would remain in the family. I can give him that, and so can you. The new will splits the property into thirds with Darryl, Miles, and Cormac getting even shares."

Darryl choked. "Cormac gets the same share that I do? And Miles when he hasn't been here?"

May gave him a stink eye so powerful he shifted back. "Miles was gone because your father made a mistake. If I split it in half between my sons, Cormac would likely get nothing because you're selfish that way. If you don't want your share, then you can give it or sell it to a McClintock, and the only three around with ties to one another are sitting at this table." She took another nibble of corn casserole and pushed her plate aside. "Emmaline, you grab that cookbook over there and take it home with you. I know you love that cornbread as much as Miles, and I hope with all my heart that you get to make it for him for years to come."

Emmaline stood and got the cookbook and held it to her heart. Looking at her, one would think she'd been given a gold bar.

"Cormac, help your gran to her bed. I'm tired." She stood and wobbled on weak legs. "Can you do me a favor? Can you all just get along until I die?" She took Cormac's arm and left the room.

They ate the rest of the meal in silence. Each time he glanced at Darryl, he felt the prick of the daggers from his brother's eyes.

As May asked, they finished their meal and cleaned the kitchen. On the drive home, Emmaline cuddled into his side. "It's so sad to see her so frail. How much time do you think she has left?"

He'd seen it all before and knew the answer was less than anyone could imagine.

CHAPTER TWENTY-THREE

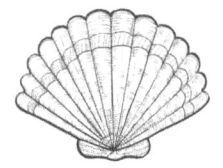

The next few days went by quickly, but that was because they were always on the run. If they weren't bringing breakfast to May, they were bringing her dinner. In between, they knocked off all the items on her list in case the critic showed up.

Em was happy that Darryl and Miles had agreed to ignore their differences for now. She hid all her shoes at night and invited Miles into her bed. In the morning, she always found Ollie with a shoe she knew she'd secured.

Mrs. Blackthorne remained like her name implied, a thorn in Em's side. Ever since the seagull incident, she'd required extra. Extra towels. Extra soap. Extra housekeeping services. Extra patience. She looked at Em with disdain and Miles like he'd saved her from a great white shark. Thankfully they were checking out this morning, and Em could be done with her for good.

Speak of the devil, Mrs. Blackthorne walked into the lobby and headed straight for Em. "I wanted to let you know that we enjoyed The Kessler. While I see you are merging the properties, I'd like to say that The Brown staff could learn something from Margot. She's adorable and friendly, whereas The Brown staff are uptight. Then there's that manager, Miles. He's just the bee's knees all the way around." She pointed her finger. "You can't tell I nearly lost it to a seagull bite." She sighed like a lovestruck teen. "That man is a keeper. I'd consider trading Harold for him, but traveling the world is a perk of Harold's job."

Em wanted to roll her eyes right after she choked the woman to death, but that wouldn't look good on a review, so she smiled.

"Thank you for staying at The Kessler. Maybe you'll try The Brown next year."

Mrs. Blackthorne shook her head. "No, we rarely stay anywhere twice. There are so many places to see."

"Yes, you're right. Please tell Mr. Blackthorne thank you and wish the girls a good week from us."

"Will do." She turned and left, and Miles walked in.

"Bet you're happy."

"That woman was a pain in my patootie. Can you believe she told me the staff at The Brown were uptight, and we should take a lesson from Margot's friendly personality?"

"She told you that?"

"Yes, and she said you were the bee's knees. She turned that barely-there break to her skin into a near amputation and nearly swooned when she spoke of how you mended her. She even spoke of trading Harold for you, but apparently, she gets to travel a lot because of his job." Her jaw went slack. "Oh no." She pulled out her phone and googled Harold Blackthorne, travel critic, but didn't get a hit. She scrolled down and came across an H. Thorne, and her heart stilled. "Oh my God. You were almost right." Miles had said he thought Diane Blackthorne was the critic, but she wasn't. "It was him."

Miles laughed. "You have to watch out for those quiet ones."

"I wonder if he knew how much his wife annoyed me." She turned toward the door, ready to bolt after Diane to see if there was anything she could offer her to make sure she was leaving on a positive note.

"I'm sure he did."

Her heartbeat took off, and her head spun. Her breath caught in her throat. The world around her twirled, and she was certain she'd faint and hit the tile floor beneath her until Miles wrapped his arms around her.

"Breathe. It's going to be okay."

"No. What if they write a terrible review?"

He rubbed her back. "Then you get a terrible review. It won't be the first or last. Shit happens."

"You don't understand. My family has been waiting for this review all their lives, and I blew it."

"You didn't blow it. Also, remember that she's not writing the review. Her husband is, and he took a liking to Margot."

"Who works at The Kessler." She stepped back, crossed her arms, and frowned. "I can't believe I didn't find him in my search."

"You were looking for Harold Blackthorne. Like a writer, he has a nom de plume. I imagine he finds some comfort in moving around anonymously."

Her stiff shoulders relaxed. "Can you imagine if people knew he was coming?"

He stared at her and grinned. "No, what would you have done differently?"

"Probably nothing."

"Then let it go. You wouldn't have known a critic was coming if Trixie hadn't posted that. Would you have seen their review?"

She nodded. "Yes, my phone is programmed to notify me when the resort gets a new review. The Brown has an excellent rating."

"Worst case, they leave a poor review, and it reflects on The Kessler, and I'll take responsibility for it. Best case, it's a shining five stars, and you can boast about teaching me all you know."

Inside, her guts twisted. She had one job her whole life: to make The Brown shine, and she might have ruined its fifteen minutes of fame because she was trying to prove a point. She knew if her parents were in heaven watching her, they weren't smiling. She'd be lucky if she weren't struck by lightning as a punishment.

"Cormac is on his way to help me finish with the painting."

"How can you afford him?" She wasn't sure how much Brie and Carter were paying him, but she was sure it wasn't enough to pay another person's salary out of his.

"I told you I have money." He looked at her with all seriousness. "I'm a regular millionaire."

She laughed. "Sure, you are." The phone rang, and she blew him a kiss. "See you later, moneybags."

Miles walked out, and she picked up the phone. "The Brown Resort Willow Bay, this is Emmaline. How can I help you?" She'd gotten used to her full name because that's all Miles called her unless he was angry, and then she was a single syllable Em. She loved the way her full name flowed from his mouth like warm honey drizzle.

"Em, this is Cormac." His voice was high-pitched and

shaky. "I tried calling Uncle Miles, but he didn't pick up. Same with Dad."

Her nerves tangled and twisted, and her heart squeezed. "What is it?" She already knew what he would say but knowing didn't make it hurt any less.

"Gran is gone." His voice broke. "I went into the living room to tell her goodbye because I was supposed to help paint today, and she had the game show network playing too loud. She was staring at the screen, mouth open, eyes open, but she wasn't there. I don't know what to do."

She hated to see anyone cry, especially a grown man. She knew the McClintocks well enough to know the men in their family weren't allowed tears, so hearing Cormac let his torrent loose broke her heart.

"I'll call Dr. Robinson. You call the sheriff. Miles and I will be there as soon as we can." She hung up and remembered that Darryl was there too.

She rushed into the kitchen, told Tilly, and then prepared to break the news to Miles. Pushing her emotions below the surface was something she was good at. She'd had a lot of practice over the years. Right now, even though her heart was breaking, she needed to be strong for Miles. He'd just gotten his mother back only to lose her to cancer.

She found him in the residence, getting ready to pour the paint into the tray.

"Wait." He must have seen the devastation on her face.

His shoulders fell forward, and the golden flecks that always danced in his eyes were snuffed out. "Does Darryl know?"

She shook her head. "Cormac tried calling both of you, but he couldn't reach either of you."

His palm skated over his forehead and fell down his face in slow motion. "I'll get Darryl. Can you feed Ollie and lock him inside? I'll meet you at the truck in less than five minutes."

She did as he asked while she dialed Dr. Robinson, who said she'd meet them there.

"Sorry, buddy," she said to the dog as she shut the door. Though she closed Ollie in the house, it was a fifty-fifty shot whether he'd stay put. Somehow, he'd figured out how to turn a handle with his mouth. He came and went as he pleased. She knew people who weren't nearly as bright.

When she left, she found Hugh shuffling along the sidewalk. "Hey, Hugh. I've got a family emergency." It wasn't a lie. Miles had become her family once again. "Can you please restock the fire pit before you leave today?"

He nodded and went on his way. Hugh may be old, but he was dependable. She could always depend on him to take four times as long and only get half of what she asked him to do done.

Miles and Darryl ran from the boathouse to the truck.

"Why is she coming?"

"Because I asked her to."

"She ain't family."

Miles opened her door and helped her inside before rounding the truck and climbing into the driver's seat. Darryl hopped into the back seat of the king cab.

"If it weren't for Dad's creative financing, she would have been my wife for thirty years already, so in my mind, she's family." He put the truck in reverse and pulled out of the parking lot. The speed limit was forty-five, but when she peeked over to look at the speedometer, Miles was doing sixty. She laid her hand on his thigh. "There's no rush, honey. What's done is done."

A whoosh of air left his lungs like he'd been holding his

breath this whole time. "It's too soon." A tear slipped down his cheek, and he swiped it away.

She pretended not to notice and took his hand in hers. "There's never enough time."

Darryl snorted. "Your timing was perfect to just swoop in and secure your inheritance.

Miles stiffened, and his free hand dropped hers and turned into a fist. "Stop." He looked over his shoulder for a fraction of a second. She didn't see his expression but was confident it was deadly. "You can have the ranch if you want it. I didn't come here for that."

Darryl leaned forward. "What did you come here for?" He poked her on the shoulder. "Mark my words. Everything he touches turns to shit. Give it time, and he'll ruin your life too."

She twisted as far as the seatbelt would allow. "Your mother just died, and all you're worried about is the damn ranch?"

"Don't pretend you don't know what I'm going through. You didn't get anything outright until everyone died too."

She didn't know what he was implying, but if it was that she had been biding her time until her entire family died so she'd get her chance at the family property, then he was delusional.

"Shut up, Darryl. You don't know me."

He laughed. "Wrong. You and I are cut from the same cloth. We want our birthright. You got the resort, and I should get the ranch. But he shows up, and what was one hundred percent mine has turned into thirty percent."

"Cormac deserves a share since he does most of the work," Miles said. "What have you done with the property in the last five years, outside of letting it deteriorate?" They drove under the sign and were on McClintock property.

"It's like the land is reclaiming itself with the four-foot grass. The main house is falling apart, and I don't even want to know what happened to the bunkhouse and cabins."

Miles came to a stop behind the sheriff's car. He killed the engine and looked at her. "You don't have to come in if you don't want to. Seeing death can be difficult."

She opened her door. "I'm going where you're going. You need me, and I'm not leaving you."

He exited, and they met at the front of the truck. "I do need you. More than I ever imagined—so much that it scares me."

She lifted on tiptoes and kissed him. It wasn't a passionate kiss, but a promise kiss. She would see him through this.

Dr. Robinson came out of the house, removing a pair of gloves. "I'm sorry for your loss. You've got a few minutes to spend with her before they take her away."

He took Emmaline's hand and led her into the house. Cormac sat on the old Barcalounger, staring straight ahead. He looked up seconds later. "There was nothing I could do."

Miles pulled him up by his hand and wrapped him in a hug. "There was nothing anyone could do. She was ready to go. You heard her last night. She said she was tired."

"Yeah, but I thought that meant she needed to sleep."

Miles hugged Cormac tighter before he stepped back. "She's taking a big sleep now."

Darryl walked in and stared at his mother, who seemed to sleep peacefully. She was no longer sitting but lying on the couch with her hand on her chest. Her eyes and mouth weren't open, as Cormac said, but closed and peaceful looking. Miles described it perfectly. May McClintock had left them for a long rest.

Within an hour, the house was cleared, and only four remained. Soon, funeral casseroles would be showing up by the dozens. People May hadn't seen in decades would talk about her like they'd had tea last Sunday.

She knew the drill. She'd buried a lot of people over the years. Hell, she probably had a few of those death casseroles still in her freezer.

"Are you hungry?" she asked.

Darryl looked at her like a toad was crawling out of her nose.

"Are you stupid?"

Miles bent over and kissed her. He reached into his pocket and took out his keys. "Honey, go home. I'll be there shortly."

"What are you going to do?"

He looked so calm. "I did what my mother asked. I kept the peace until she passed, but now, I'm going to kick Darryl's ass. Cormac? I'll need a ride to the hospital or the resort when I'm done. Can I count on you to have my back?"

Cormac looked at his uncle and then his father. He shook his head. "I'm not taking sides." He pointed to a hook on the wall where a set of keys hung. "Whoever is left standing can take my truck." He rose from the lounger and addressed her. "You ready to go?"

She walked to the door. "Protect those lips, baby. I love your kisses."

"You got it, sweetheart." She heard the first punch hit before she walked out the door. "Do you think they'll be okay?"

Cormac shrugged. "I don't know, but this is a long time coming. Who do you think will win?"

CHAPTER TWENTY-FOUR

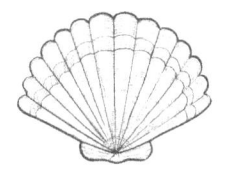

Darryl landed the first punch, but that was how Miles wanted it to happen. He'd told him that if he hit him again, he'd make sure Darryl couldn't use that arm for some time.

"Let's take it outside. This is Mom's house, and she never allowed fighting inside." She may be gone, but she wasn't forgotten, and her rules would ring in his ears for years to come.

As soon as they cleared the porch, Darryl rushed him and knocked him to the dirt. He got one more slug in before Miles let loose. Years of unleashed pent-up torment and anger hailed forward, and it wasn't long before Darryl called a truce.

They separated and sat on opposite ends of the porch steps catching their breath and releasing the trapped endorphins in labored breaths and groans.

"Why are you such an asshole?" Miles asked.

Darryl shrugged and grimaced as if the action brought him pain. "Maybe it's because nothing I do turns out right."

He wiped his bloody nose on the back of his hand. "Even my son seems to like you better."

The last thing he wanted to do was come between father and son. "Maybe that's because you're an a—"

"I know, I'm an asshole."

He remembered what Emmaline said and repeated her words. "At least we agree on something."

"What are we going to do with the place?"

Miles thought back to his mother's words. "The property has to stay in McClintock hands. So, we have to work together."

Darryl squeezed his eyes tight and scrubbed his hand over his face. "It costs money to run a place like this, and frankly, I'm not interested in working that hard. If you or Cormac had the money, I'd sell it to you and walk away, but I know Cormac doesn't have a dime, and you ... I can't imagine you have much either."

"How much do you want?"

"What?" Darryl brushed the dirt off his jeans. "You win the lottery?"

Miles's shoulders shook with his laughter. He wasn't about to tell his brother he was right. "I've got some money put away."

Darryl stared at the land in front of him. "The buildings aren't worth much. A hard wind might take them down. The land is worth millions. I'd say my share is about two and a half million."

Miles looked around and knew his brother couldn't see the value of the property, but Miles saw it through his and Emmaline's eyes from thirty years ago. They used to ride horses and dream of a tourist ranch where they could do cattle drives, horseback rides, and chuck-wagon dinners.

"If I gave you two and a half million dollars to walk away, would you?"

His brother gawked at him before rolling his eyes. "You're offering me millions to sign over my ranch share?"

He didn't want to tip his hand just yet, but he wanted to plant the seed. "Let's just pretend I had that kind of money."

"Oh, I see. This is just pretending. Okay then. My pretend answer would be yes. I'd give it to you for a million. Hell, I'd probably pay you to take it. Who wants a legacy weighing them down?"

He'd been disconnected from his family's legacy for decades and missed it. "What would you do?"

Darryl whistled and smiled. "First, I'd get drunk, and then I'd buy myself a brand-new truck, and I'd travel. I've never left the state of Texas. Hell, as far as I know, there's nothing past its borders."

He understood. He hadn't left the state until they kicked him off the ranch. "I can guarantee there's a world beyond Texas."

"It's good that Mom isn't around to hear such blasphemy." A sadness fell over Darryl, and Miles imagined he was crying on the inside where it was allowed.

For Miles, he'd already processed the death of his family long ago. That didn't mean he wasn't feeling its permanence, but he'd mourned their loss all those years ago.

"Are you going to be okay?"

Darryl nodded. "It'll take some getting used to." Then he smiled. "But my earlobes are grateful."

Miles rose from the step. "Are you returning to the resort or staying here?"

Darryl drug himself up by the handrail. "I think it's too

soon to stay here alone. I'll think about her laying there with *The Price is Right* playing in the background."

"Let me get the keys. I'll meet you at Cormac's truck." Miles entered the house. It smelled like dusty curtains and death. Anyone who told him death didn't have a smell had never experienced it. It was sadness, anger, and unfulfilled dreams mixed and left in the sun to rot. Love gone wrong, unresolved family disputes, and dreams died on the tip of a tongue because things like lack of money or time stole them. Death was a reminder of how precious life was. Each time he experienced it, he reminded himself that his only purpose was to love and live.

He took the keys from the hook and gave the house a final glance. "Goodbye, Mama. I'll miss you." He swiped away the tear running down his cheek and closed the door behind him.

The drive was mostly silent until Darryl asked, "You and Emmaline back together?"

After this week, he could solidly say yes. "We make a great team."

Darryl nodded. "I always thought so. I was jealous of what you two had. I never had that."

"I thought you and Sherry were in love." He didn't want to point out that Cormac was born six months after they wed.

"I loved her, but it wasn't the kind of love that soaks into your cells. How did you stay away for all these years?"

"Mostly, it was self-preservation. It's easier to do without something if it's not there tempting you every day." He drove through Main Street and turned onto the coastal highway. "Are we okay?" He knew he and Darryl would never be close. His father had ensured that, but maybe they could be in the same room and not want to kill one another.

"I'll always dislike you, but I think for Mom's sake, I'll tolerate you." He shifted his jaw. "Where did you learn how to punch like that?"

Miles glanced at him. "I learned from you."

He rubbed his chin. "I taught you too damn well."

"It was an on-the-job learning experience." It seemed like all they did as kids was fight, and being the older brother, Darryl had the upper hand. He was bigger, meaner, and had more experience. "Clean up, and I'll treat you to room service."

Darryl laughed. "I won't be a cheap date. I see a lot of expensive alcohol and a steak coming my way."

"I can afford you."

"That's right. You won the lottery."

"Yes, I did." That was the first time he had admitted it, but Darryl thought he was still pretending. "You think about that offer, okay?"

"Right." They exited Cormac's truck and walked to the Kessler.

Miles followed Darryl inside and found Margot standing at the front desk. He pointed to his brother. "Can you get him some tattered towels, so he doesn't ruin the good ones?"

She looked at both of them. "My Lord. What happened to the two of you?"

"Just settling an old score," Miles said. "By the way, he might be coming into some money soon."

Margot smiled. "Well then, let me make sure you've got everything you need."

Darryl stared at him. "You were joking, right? You didn't win, did you?"

Miles walked out of The Kessler without answering. He returned to the residence, where he had a lot of work to do before Carter and Brie returned from their honeymoon.

Emmaline showed up just after he showered and was putting the first coat of paint on the bedroom wall. She leaned against the doorframe. "Are you okay?"

He sighed. "I will be. The thing about death is we are headed there the moment we're born. You learn to appreciate each day a little more when you accept that." He set his roller down and pulled her into his arms. "I love you, Emmaline, and I don't want a day to go by that you don't hear me say it."

"I love you too. We owe each other close to eleven thousand extra I love yous. That's how many we missed while you were gone."

He kissed her, spilling all the day's emotions into her mouth, and she accepted his grief and sadness and filled him with love and hope. When she pulled away, she looked at him with such love that he wanted to weep.

"I can help you finish," she offered.

He loved that she would, but he knew she was swamped. "Don't you have work at the resort?"

"I do, but you're more important."

"How about you do what you have to, and I'll finish up here? I'll probably be late, but I'll be there."

She pushed off the wall and gingerly touched the corner of his eye. "You're going to have a black eye by morning. You should ice this."

"Yes, ma'am."

She laughed. "That makes me feel old."

He nuzzled her neck. "When I climb in bed with you tonight, I'll make you feel young again."

She faked a shiver. "Should I wear something sexy?"

He thought back to his and Margot's conversation about

teddies. "Do you still have that red number you had way back when?"

She shook her head. "No, but I have flannel pajamas and rabbit slippers."

"I think Ollie stole one of them."

She sighed. "He did. I found it on the stairs to The Brown a while back."

"Speaking of Ollie, where is he?"

She grinned. "I've got him cleaning all my left shoes. He's very good at it." They walked to the door. "Now that you own a third of a ranch, what will you do with it?"

He wasn't sure, but he had a few ideas. Emmaline was married to the resort, but that didn't mean they couldn't expand. "How would you feel about owning another resort?"

Her eyes grew wide. "Do you know how hard that would be? Besides, you'd have to get rid of Darryl because he's not resort-running material, and that would mean paying him off."

"Can we talk tonight? I've got some things I need to tell you."

"Should I be worried?"

In what world would being rich worry anyone? "Nope. You'll be happy."

She gave him another kiss. This one was too short but seemed to promise more later. "Finish the paint job, and I'll see if I can't round up something sexier than flannel."

He went back to work and spent the next several hours finishing the painting and moving the furniture back in place. He was dog-tired when he locked up the house and started for Emmaline's. Noise from the beach drew his attention, and he saw that a group had started a bonfire. He hadn't realized how much time had passed, but it was well past dark. When he walked inside Emmaline's, Ollie was at the door to greet him. In his mouth was a bunny slipper.

"You wrapped her around your finger, didn't you, boy?" Every muscle in his body ached as he trudged up the stairs. When he entered what had become their room, he found Emmaline fast asleep. Rather than wake her, he undressed and climbed into bed beside her. As he drifted off to sleep, he couldn't help but think that all the bad was behind them. All they had left was forever.

CHAPTER TWENTY-FIVE

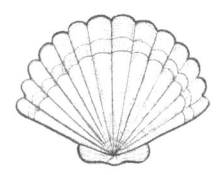

Emmaline woke to Ollie's barking, the smell of smoke, and the shrill of a fire alarm. She threw back the covers and realized the room was hazy. "Miles!" She always set the next day's clothes out the night before and reached for her pants. "Miles!" she yelled again. "Get up! Something is burning." Ollie was beside himself. It was the first time she'd seen him without a shoe in his mouth. He danced around the room in a panic.

"What the hell?" Miles was up and jumped straight into his pants before he ran to the door. "Get out of the house." They raced out the bedroom door, only to meet thicker smoke and enough heat to blister their skin, but she didn't see flames. "Stay low and breathe through your shirt." He took her hand and led her down the stairs and out the front door. Ollie barked and whined while circling their legs as if he was telling them all about the fire.

Outside, the situation was more dire than she thought. Flames licked at the clapboard siding of the house.

She turned to find Miles calling 911 and running into the main resort to help the guests to a safer area.

"Oh my God, the guests." She took off toward The Brown to help people down the stairs and to the parking lot.

Tilly ran out of the kitchen with a fire extinguisher in her hand, but it would be useless in this situation. "What the hell happened?"

"I don't know. What time is it?"

Tilly looked at her phone. "I made Hugh a pot of coffee about an hour ago, around five-thirty. He said he came in early because Mabel had a doctor's appointment. He looked tired."

She glanced around and saw Hugh standing in the driveway with the others. Relief washed through her knowing he was safe. She could replace a building, but she couldn't replace a life. The sirens wailed in the distance as she watched everything she'd worked for burn to the ground. While her family's legacy died, she couldn't grieve because she had guests to attend to. When her staff showed up for their shifts, she put them to work opening the second floor of The Kessler. Tilly sent several of her cooks into town to get supplies, and she moved her operation into The Kessler's restaurant. It wasn't ideal, but it was all they could offer, and most guests were grateful. By the time the fire was out, all that remained was a shell of the building and the six fully intact bungalows.

She'd been too busy to cry, but now that it was all calming down, she sat on the picnic bench and bawled. Her father always thought she'd burn the place down, and while she didn't set the fire, she felt just as responsible.

"Hey." Miles arrived with a plate of fruit and cheese. "You haven't eaten anything."

"I feel sick to my stomach."

Minutes later, Darryl arrived and sat next to Miles. "I'm so sorry this happened."

She glared at him. "Do you know how it started?" She hated the accusation in her voice, but she'd been thinking about the fire all day and wondered if Darryl had anything to do with it.

"Do you think I did it?" He threw his hands into the air. "I'd never do that."

"You are mad at your brother, and I imagine you don't want to see him succeed."

He shook his head. "I'm an asshole, but not that kind. You're right, I don't want him to succeed where I can't, but I'd never ruin what you have."

She looked at the smoldering ash. "Had."

Miles wrapped his arm around her shoulder. "I thought you might blame me."

"You? Why would I blame you?"

"Because I asked you to give up the resort and come away with me."

She leaned into him. "It was a hypothetical question."

"Like when you asked me if I'd sell you the ranch?" His brother cocked his head. "Did you win the lotto and burn down her resort, so she'd have to leave it and follow your dreams?"

"Lotto?" She turned to face Miles. "What's he talking about?"

Miles looked between her and Darryl. "Okay, let me explain something before you jump to conclusions. Remember when you asked me why The Kessler, and I said I was talking to Carter about it, and you assumed I was talking about managing it? I was looking to buy it."

Her jaw went slack. "But you're managing it. Besides, how could you afford a property like this?" Her eyes went wide. "Oh my God. You actually won the lotto?"

He nodded. "I did."

"I want five million for my share of the ranch," Darryl said.

"Deal, now go away." Darryl got up, and Miles turned back to her. "That day I saw you in the hospital, I knew we weren't finished, so I did what I had to do to get close to you. Carter and Brie weren't sure they wanted to sell, and they weren't sure I'd want to buy, so they asked me to manage it as a 'try before you buy' deal while they were on their honeymoon."

She stared at him and tried to process everything he was telling her. He was rich.

"Why didn't you tell me?"

She watched him take three deep breaths. "When you turned me away all those years ago, I thought it was because I had lost everything and only had my love to offer. If you were going to love me now, I didn't want my newly gained windfall to be the reason."

She took his hand. "I didn't let you go because you were poor. Leaving without a cent was worrying, but I didn't go with you because I was an idiot. I put more value into my parents' dream than I did mine. There's been no one but you, Miles. When you left, you took my heart with you, and I didn't feel whole until the day you returned."

"Did you think that I might have burned The Brown down to get you to leave it?"

"No," she lied. She would like to say the thought hadn't entered her mind, but it had, even though it was a ridiculous notion. There was no way Miles would ruin her life just to improve his. It wasn't in his nature. "What do I do now?"

"Nothing. Just let it soak in and mourn the loss. I'm sure Brie and Carter will let us stay with them until you decide what you want to do. Insurance should probably cover a rebuild, but if it doesn't, I'll cover the costs."

"Wow, I keep forgetting I have a rich boyfriend."

He took both of her hands in his. "I don't want to be your boyfriend, Emmaline."

Her heart stopped beating. Was this where he realized she came with too much baggage? Maybe he finally understood that she was nothing without The Brown. It defined who she was, and now that it was gone, she wasn't sure where she fit in. "You're breaking up with me?"

He laughed so loud that it scared the seagulls on the beach into flight. "Are you kidding? I gave you up once. I'm never giving you up again. I don't want you as a girlfriend. I want you as a wife."

She sat up straight. "Are you asking me to marry you?"

He brought her hands to his lips and kissed both. "I don't have a ring, but I can buy you whatever you want."

"I don't need a ring."

He shook his head. "Oh yes, you do. I want everyone who sees your left hand to know you're taken. Hell, I'd tattoo 'Property of Miles McClintock' across your forehead if you'd let me."

"No way, all tattoos fade over time, and I don't look good in faded colors. I only wore that pale pink the other day to make you regret you left me. In truth, I've grown into a jewel tone girl."

"If I remember correctly, your color is diamond."

Despite the sadness that threatened to overwhelm her, she laughed. "I don't know how you can make me smile when I've lost everything."

He thumbed up her chin, so she was looking into his eyes. "You lost nothing. This is all stuff, and it can be replaced. We have each other, and that's everything."

A shadow fell over them, and when she looked up, she saw Carter and Brie.

"When we left, I knew you two hotheads would battle it out, but I never thought you'd burn the place down," Brie said. She kneeled and pulled Emmaline in for a hug. "I'm sorry about the loss."

Carter looked behind him and smiled. "I guess this means The Kessler just moved into the number one spot to stay in Willow Bay."

Brie slugged him in the arm. "How can you joke when my aunt just lost everything?"

Emmaline took a minute to process what she wanted to say. "Everything is right here." She stared at what was left. "Who we are was never in that building. Never forget that. We can rebuild if you want." She turned to Brie. "You're a half owner."

Brie laughed. "Half owner of nothing is still nothing."

She knew Brie was never invested in the resort and said, "We're insured."

Brie took a seat at the picnic bench. "Do you want to rebuild?"

CHAPTER TWENTY-SIX

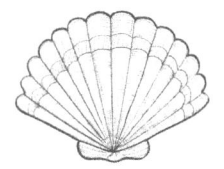

Over the next few days, Miles helped Emmaline sift through the rubble. The funny thing about fire was it seemed selective at times and completely indiscriminate at others. The entire house had been reduced to a pile of rubbish with the exception of the hall closet that held all the family photo albums. Once the ash had cooled and the fire department said it was okay, she opened the door to find a footlocker full of family mementos. Miles picked it up and carried it to the picnic table.

"Unbelievable," she said as she tugged at the handle to open it. The heat from the fire had charred the hinges, but the lid popped free, and she pulled out pictures that dated back to when her grandparents bought the property. She peeled one from the top.

The only sign that the photos had been through a fire was the acrid smoky smell that seemed to soak into everything and the mustiness of paper that had met with dampness.

"Is that the land before anything was built?" He took

the old black and white photo from her hand and held it up. He could line it up with landmark trees like the giant willow that still stood in the center of the property.

"It would seem so. Look how pretty and pure it all seems." She ran her finger over the photo of the beach and the sand. "This was before it was touched with greed and ego."

He laid the photo down and looked into her eyes. "I know you were too emotionally spent to answer Brie the other day when she asked if you wanted to rebuild but what about now? You've had a few days to digest the loss." He leaned in and kissed her gently. "Before you answer, I want you to know that I'll support you in anything you want to do. My place is beside you."

She swiped a tear from her cheek. It couldn't be easy losing everything she held dear. Her dreams had revolved around The Brown since the beginning of time. He knew what she was going through. Though the ranch had never burned down, it had been ripped away from him when he was younger. The property might not have turned to ashes, but his life had gone up in flames. He'd lost everything, and yet, he recovered. He knew she would as well.

"Everything I thought I was, and everything I wanted to be, was wrapped up in this property." When he went to dispute her claim, and tell her she was not The Brown, she raised her hand. "Let me finish." She cleared her throat. "This land was a legacy of love for my ancestors. They came here to rest and relax. That was its original intent. It was a vacation home for a wealthy family. Then my family stepped in and turned the place on its head. It was still a place for people to come and unwind but not for The Browns. They took something beautiful and peaceful and turned it into a place where ego and money ruled. Look at the misery this place has caused. It took two lovers and created a divide so wide that they could never cross it to live their dream. They had to live a lie to survive. My poor sister was torn between her love of Cyrus and her loyalty to The Brown. I wasn't much different. I should have left with you that day, but guilt for the decades of work my ancestors put into this place held me back. This just proves that a heart can't be divided. I should have let the romantic in me rule my world. Love for you should have been my guiding light."

"Hindsight is always 20/20," he said.

"Too bad we can't always have the clarity that a disaster brings."

Ollie bound down the cement steps that used to lead to the front desk and ran to where they sat at the picnic table. In his mouth was a half-charred bunny slipper—the left one.

"Ollie seems to have his priorities set."

In the distance, Brie and Carter walked out of The Kessler and toward them.

"Are you okay?" Brie asked as she approached.

Emmaline nodded. "I will be. It's a lot to take in but Miles and I were discussing clarity, and I think for the first time in my life, I'm really clear on what I want and what I don't."

Brie's eyes widened. "Have you made a decision?"

Miles couldn't wait to hear what she'd say. He'd watched her sink into silent contemplation the last few days. He was always by her side but knew he couldn't help influence her decision. If she chose The Brown this time, it was because she wanted to prove something to herself and not to her family. She'd already chosen him by saying yes to his marriage proposal, so he'd support her no matter what.

He didn't care if he spent his life at The Brown, The Kessler, or the ranch. All he cared about was spending the rest of his days with Emmaline.

"What's on your mind sweetheart?"

CHAPTER TWENTY-SEVEN

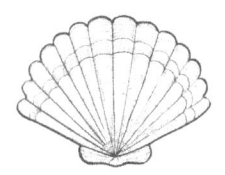

Em looked around the property. "To rebuild or not to rebuild ." That has been the question on everyone's minds, including hers. Em's attention went from the burned down Brown Resort to The Kessler, which now stood proud. It was funny to imagine a property having a personality, but somehow, The Kessler seemed happier now that The Brown was gone. The paint seemed brighter, the foliage greener, the flowers more vibrant. The guests they had moved from The Brown seemed quite content to be shifted over to a new resort where they were spoiled by Em's staff, Carter, and Brie.

With the help of Charlotte and Marybeth, no one was missing essentials as her two friends hit the community up for whatever the guests needed from clothes to amenities like makeup and books. Tilly was out of sorts since The Kessler kitchen was substandard in her opinion, but there was no doubt in Em's mind that her feisty friend would whip it into shape in no time.

When Miles reached for her hand, she realized they were all waiting on her to answer. She opened her mouth to say the words, but they seemed to lodge in her throat. Turning her attention away from The Brown seemed the right thing to do. It wasn't that owning a resort was a bad thing, but since the fire she'd come to realize that the Brown family never truly owned the resort, it owned them. A life lived for someone and something else was never truly a life lived. The biggest conclusion she came to was that she never truly wanted the resort. What she wanted was to be seen and valued and appreciated. Somehow that basic need had gotten tied up into the success of the business. Hindsight truly gave you perfect vision because all along she'd been seen ... by her friends, her niece, her townsfolk, and by Miles. They loved her whether she succeeded or not. What she learned this week was to see herself. She didn't need a thriving business to make her whole. Her friends were right. The Brown would never warm her bed, bring her coffee in the morning, or hold her when she was down.

She considered her answer for another moment before she swallowed the lump in her throat. "No."

Miles gasped. "What do you mean?"

"This was never my dream. I have another dream that includes a cowboy, a ranch, and a shoe-stealing dog." She looked deep into his eyes. "What do you say?"

Miles nodded. "I think that's a fine idea."

Carter sat next to Brie. "We haven't had a lot of time to catch up since we hit the ground running. I can't help but feel like we missed a lot while we were gone."

Em nodded. The only information that was passed to the newlyweds was there was a fire. Since then, they'd been busy keeping guests happy. Em spent the last few days coming to grips with her loss. She hadn't even told her niece about the engagement. "You did miss a lot and I'm so sorry that I've been so self-absorbed."

Brie shook her head. "It's understandable. We figured we'd let you have a few days to yourself but then we saw you outside and thought we'd join you."

Em sat up and smiled. "I'm glad you did because there's so much to share. Here is the short version: Your meddling worked. Miles and I fell in love again. In fact, we're getting married." She looked at Miles. "He's the kindest, most giving man I've ever met. He proposed the day the resort burned down." She rubbed the empty place on her ring finger. "I think he did that so the day wouldn't be remembered as the worst day of my life." She looked at him. "You still want to marry me, right?"

"Emmaline, you own my heart. It's always belonged to you. There is no place I'd rather be than right here next to you." He stared down at her hand. "As soon as we're finished here, we're putting a ring on that finger so finish up your story, love. We've got some shopping to do."

She giggled and tried to put the sentences in a succinct order. "May passed, and somehow, we burned down the resort. Oh, and a travel critic stayed at The Kessler. You'll have to blame Miles if the review is bad because he was in charge."

Both of their eyes got as wide as butter plates. "Oh, is that all?" Brie asked.

Miles smiled and pulled back his shoulders. "Nope, I won the lottery." He reached over and shook Carter's hand. "I'd love to stay and manage your place, but if Emmaline is open to the idea of running a dude ranch, I'd like to pursue that." He turned to look at her. Hope and love filled his expression.

"That's a big commitment," she said.

"Baby, I'm all in. Whatever it takes, we'll build our dream."

"I'm not talking about the ranch. That part is easy, but I fear I'm not."

Everyone at the table nodded.

"No, but you're worth it."

Not many people got a do-over, but she was getting one, and she wouldn't pass it up. How many people got a second chance at their only true love?

"Now that that's settled" Carter said. "It would seem we have new competition. I'll look forward to it. Anything else we should know?"

Emmaline shrugged. "Nothing that you don't already. You're fully staffed, and Tilly is running your kitchen. She'd like to call it Edelweiss and serve her famous German food. I hate to bail on you, but like Miles said, we've got some shopping to do." She looked under the table where Ollie lay on her feet. "Oh, and Ollie may seem like a very good boy, but he has a bad habit. Hide your shoes."

"Wait," Brie said. "Is that why I'm missing all my left shoes?"

CHAPTER TWENTY-EIGHT

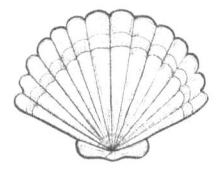

Miles sat in the booth across from Emmaline and watched as she stared at the insurance check. It had been a month since the fire, and all the investigations were complete. The cause was listed as hot embers that caught fire in the dumpster on the backside of Emmaline's house.

The insurance adjuster valuated the property at several million. Tilly said it was because she had a top-notch kitchen, but it was because Emmaline kept impeccable records stored on the Cloud.

"It's hard to believe that a life's worth of work comes down to this. I mean, it's a big check, but it's a hundred years of my ancestors' blood, sweat, and tears."

Miles couldn't argue with that. The Brown had been in her family since the early 1900s. "What are you going to do with it?"

"Half is Brie's. I tried to give her the whole thing, but she wouldn't take it."

"What will you do with your half?"

"I'm giving a couple of hundred thousand to Hugh.

Even though he started the fire, he didn't mean to. I thought I was doing him a favor by giving him a job, but giving him a nice nest egg that will cover Mabel's QVC obsession is the right thing to do."

He couldn't argue with that. It was time for Hugh to take a break and enjoy what life he had left.

After the death of his father and his mother, he was reminded that life was too short to waste time on the small things and just about everything, but love was a small thing. "What else?"

"I've got a wedding to plan."

They had decided to wait until they built a main house on the McClintock ranch to get married. They didn't need a piece of paper telling them they were together. They'd always been together, even when they were apart. That didn't stop him from putting a giant diamond on her finger the day they went shopping. They might know they belonged together, but that ring would signal the message to everyone else that she belonged to him.

"Put that thing away." Cricket walked over carrying a pot of coffee and an order pad. "You can blind a girl with so much bling."

Emmaline smiled and looked at her ring. "It is enormous and blindingly shiny."

"Only the best for my girl," Miles said.

Cricket scooted into the booth next to Emmaline and kicked her feet up on the seat next to him. On the bottom of her shoe, drawn in thin, black, permanent marker, was a middle finger.

"Are you tired, or is that for me?" He stared at it again. It seemed freshly drawn.

"Oh, that's for you all right. I hear you're a millionaire, and the last time you dined in my fine establishment, you left me a twenty percent tip." She made a throaty growl. "Cheap bastard." She turned to Emmaline. "You need to teach this boy that when you have more, you give more. He needs to tip better."

Emmaline smiled. "Yes, ma'am. I'll do my best, but some men are hard to train."

Cricket glanced under the table at Ollie. "I bet he'd leave me a bigger tip than you."

Miles laughed. "Right after he stole your shoes."

Cricket cocked her head. "You think he knows what happened to my blue high-tops? I left them by the door after the morning shift, and one day the left one was gone. Who takes just one shoe?"

Miles stared at his dog. "Ollie?"

The pup covered his head with his paws.

"I think we owe you a pair of high-tops," Emmaline said. "How about one in each color of the rainbow?"

Cricket smiled. "Will you draw the finger on them for me? My arthritis has been acting up."

Emmaline reached for the honey. "Put this on it. It's a cure-all."

Cricket grinned. "I knew you listened to me. Now, what will it be?"

Miles looked at the menu and then pushed it aside. "Do we get a choice?"

Cricket laughed. "Not really, but I like for you to think you do. Two blue-plate specials are coming up."

Emmaline raised four fingers. "Make it four. We're expecting guests." Just as she said it, the door opened, and in walked Brie and Carter.

Cricket rose from the booth, and the two filled in the empty seats. In Carter's hand were the plans for the open space left behind by the fire. In Brie's, was the local paper. Miles caught a glimpse of Trixie's Travels headline.

"Which should we see first, the plans or the critic's review?" Miles asked.

Emmaline sat up straight. "It posted?"

Brie smiled. "It did. Do you want to see it?"

"Do I?" Emmaline appeared uncertain, but in the end, she nodded. "Just rip the Band-Aid off quickly."

Brie cleared her throat and began reading Trixie's Travels article.

"Dear Traveler,

"This week's travel review is of one of our own. As you know, nothing is hotter than a Texas summer except maybe the week The Brown Resort burned down. Sadly, this review is a posthumous nod to The Brown and a pat on the back to its neighbor, The Kessler. Without further ado, here's what H. Thorne had to say about our little town.

"The Thornes have been at it again, only this time, we went coastal which is a far better experience than going postal. (A little disgruntled postal service worker humor for you.) We were blessed to land in the quaint little town of Willow Bay where, outside of camping and staying at an Airbnb, there are two options. Visitors either come to The Kessler or The Brown. If you wait too long to reserve, you don't have much choice. You get The Kessler. At first, we were disappointed to stay there as we wanted to experience one of the lovely bungalows on The Brown property. It's widely known the two resorts have been in competition since both families broke ground. However, what greeted us was a surprise. We were able to get the best of both worlds as The Brown and The Kessler have joined forces. No bungalow for us, but we had a warm, friendly staff managed by Miles McClintock and access to the culinary magic of chef Tilly

Beck, who runs the kitchen at The Brown. Emmaline Brown educated us on the local wildlife. We were as happy as a flock of seagulls pecking at a plate of quiche. Next time you're heading south, put Willow Bay on your itinerary and stop in at The Brown and The Kessler and tell them the Thornes sent you."

Brie smiled. "They gave us four and a half stars."

"I taught Miles everything he knows," Emmaline said.

Miles laughed. "Maybe we would have gotten five stars if you hadn't fed her to the seagulls."

Emmaline's shoulders shook. "Maybe Mr. Blackthorne would have insisted we get ten if we let the birds carry his wife away."

"That sounds like a story we'll want to hear," Carter said. "Hopefully they'll come back, and they can stay in one of the new bungalows."

"You're building new bungalows?" Emmaline asked.

"Let me show you." Carter rolled the plans out and pointed at the area which used to be the house. "Brie and I have talked about what we'd like to see happen to the land. And since you're half-owner, Aunt Em, we'd like your approval."

Emmaline took a folder from her bag. "I never got around to giving you a wedding present." She removed the quitclaim deed to her half of the property and handed it to them. "Build your dreams but don't make them your children's. Be kind and generous, and always give more than you take. If you ever get to a point when all things seem lost, look into each other's eyes, and rekindle the love you found there that moment when you decided they were the one." She handed the deed over. "Now show us what you've got planned."

They discussed building more bungalows and a playground for the kids that they wanted to name after Olivia. Since they didn't need two boathouses, they would expand the beach area and tear down The Kessler's. Because the restaurant at The Kessler was smaller than Tilly wanted, they gave her free rein to expand.

"You know I'm giving her half a million dollars, right? She might take that and build her own place."

Miles didn't know she was giving Tilly half a million dollars until that second, but he couldn't think of anyone more deserving. When he thought about loyalty, Tilly was the poster child.

"What about Charlotte and Marybeth?" He knew she wouldn't do for one and not the others.

"Oh, I'll donate to the church and make a sizeable cash donation to Charlotte's new project."

"Which is?" he asked.

Emmaline smiled. "She's the town's new wedding planner, and we're her first clients."

"Should I be worried?"

She nodded. "Terrified."

CHAPTER TWENTY-NINE

TWO MONTHS LATER.

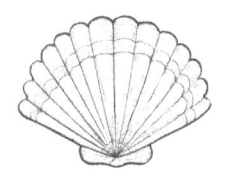

It was shocking how fast a house could be built when you had money. Emmaline stood outside the big ranch-style home with the wraparound porch and smiled. It was finished and furnished, but they hadn't moved in. Miles wanted to wait until their wedding night—tonight.

On the lawn out front was an enormous white tent where no less than twenty-five tables, decked out with flowers and Sweet on You candies, sat waiting for guests. Charlotte wanted to make an impression and went all out. In the center of the tent was an enormous ice sculpture, because nothing said I love you like two six-foot swans with their necks intertwined to form a heart. In Texas, bigger was always better.

Charlotte arrived and dragged two suitcases from the trunk of her car. "Get inside before he sees you," she said. "It's bad luck for the groom to see the bride on her wedding day."

"It's his wedding day too, and he's not even here." She had to sleep in Charlotte's spare bedroom because there were specific arguments that she knew she'd never win.

Sleeping with her fiancé two night before the wedding was allowed, but the night before was against the rules. Since Charlotte didn't want her makeup job glistening off on the ride over, she left Em in the ranch house with a cup of hot tea and went back to get her supplies. "Do I need two suitcases to make me look presentable?"

Charlotte ignored her last question while she dragged her bags inside and set up in the kitchen. "He's not here because it won't take him four hours to get ready."

"Why is it going to take four hours? I bet Miles is still sleeping off his bachelor party."

"Tilly made sure she had a gallon of coffee brewed so he'd be sober for the big day."

Why they held bachelor parties the night before the event was beyond her. "Seriously? Four hours and two suitcases full of beauty products? You realize he's seen me at my worst."

Charlotte nodded and smiled. "But has he seen you at your best?"

"I hope so. Either way, I don't think he cares. All he wants is to marry me."

"Did he ask you to sign a prenup?"

"What? No. That's not who we are."

"Good because I have Tilly on speed dial to do something awful like over-salt his eggs if he did something stupid." She pointed to the table. "You know the drill. First a facial. There will be a little hellfire before we get to heaven."

"Do we have to—" Emmaline didn't finish the sentence before Charlotte slapped the goop on her face and her skin heated. Since she'd lived through it once and saw the benefits. It was easier the second time around.

It wouldn't have taken all four hours, but Charlotte

disappeared for lengths of time, making sure everything was perfect. Charlotte didn't realize that the day could have been just Emmaline and Miles alone under the sun or stars, and it would have been flawless. Her niece showed up to spend time with her while Marybeth and Tilly did everything Charlotte demanded. Her reputation as a wedding planner rested on this event.

Charlotte rushed in. "The guests are here and we're almost ready." Poor Charlotte looked ready to faint and take flight at the same time.

Emmaline looked down at her slip. "Do you think I should put on my dress?"

The look on Charlotte's face was priceless. "Oh, my God, you're not even dressed."

Marybeth walked in with Tilly. They were wearing pink dresses in the same hue but in different styles. "Why aren't you dressed?" Marybeth asked. "The pastor is waiting for you, and so is Miles."

Her heart took off like it was running down the aisle and had left her body behind. "Miles is waiting for me?"

Tilly shook her head. "Girl, get your dress on and get out there. He's been waiting for thirty years; don't make him wait for thirty more."

Charlotte removed the ivory lace dress from its hanger and slipped it over Emmaline's head, careful not to displace the updo she had painstakingly pinned in place.

Brie walked down the hallway looking perplexed. "I'm sorry, Charlotte. I can't find it anywhere."

"Find what?" Emmaline asked. She hoped no one had lost their wedding rings.

They stared at Brie. "Your left shoe is missing."

Emmaline laughed so hard she cried. Charlotte had a

conniption and pointed out that the damn dog was ruining her masterpiece.

When "Better Today" played, she didn't have time to care about her shoe. She grabbed her flowers and headed for the door.

"There are rules," Charlotte reminded her. She set the crown of wildflowers on top of Emmaline's head. "Don't forget. A lady never looks too eager."

"Charlotte, get it together, or I'm leaving everyone behind."

"Fine." Charlotte lined everyone up, and by the second verse, Em was on her way, barefoot and all. As she brought up the end of the procession, she thought about all the ceremonial prerequisites for a bride. Something old was a handkerchief Miles found in May's drawer and was now tucked inside her bra. New was the dress she found at a discount bridal shop. Just because she could afford couture didn't mean she needed it or wanted it. Blue was the morning glories that cascaded from her bouquet. And borrowed … she hadn't checked off that item until her left shoe went missing. She supposed she could twist the rules and say that Ollie borrowing her shoe fit the bill.

When she got to Miles, he looked handsome, wearing his tuxedo and black cowboy hat. She wanted to skip all the words and rush him into the house to start the wedding night, but everyone had gone to a lot of trouble to make sure this day was perfect.

Next to Miles was Darryl, who had become less judgmental and a lot kinder now that he had five million dollars in the bank. Cormac was there too. He opted to keep a lesser share of the ranch and cashed out a percentage of his ownership, so he'd have some money. As she looked at him, she saw he only had eyes for Tiffany and her daughter, Ava, who'd shown up to deliver candy and stayed to enjoy the festivities. Rumor had it that she was back with her ex-husband which broke her heart for Cormac.

Marybeth's husband, Raleigh, who she only referred to as the pastor, cleared his throat and started the ceremony. They went for the traditional vows. Although she knew Raleigh was talking, she didn't hear a word he said. Miles silently conveyed all the words she needed to hear with his eyes. They said I love you. I will worship you. I'm here with you.

CARE to find out what happens when the town's new wedding planner meets the man of her dreams? The only problem is, he's marrying someone else. *Because You Said Yes* is up next.

SNEAK PEEK - BROKEN HART
NOAH

Cross Creek wasn't a metropolis, but with a population of 2,500, I should have been able to escape three of the residents—my brothers—at least for a single night.

Sitting at a table in Roy's Bar, amongst many of the other less annoying residents, I brought my beer to my lips as my brothers entered and walked my way. Quinn dropped into the seat beside me. Ethan and Bayden—Quinn's fraternal twin—sat across the table and signaled for beers.

Quinn clapped me on the back. "You're extra broody tonight." I lifted both shoulders, then let them sag as if the strain of a dozen bags of concrete weighted them down. This time of year always hit me hard, and it amazed me that my brothers didn't get it.

"I'm not broody."

"He totally is," Quinn spoke directly to Bayden, who ignored both of us as Angie walked by. Bayden leaned over, watching the sway of her hips as she passed.

"Don't even think about it." Ethan lifted his gaze from his tablet, where he was likely jotting down ideas for our next big construction project and looked at Bayden. He snapped his fingers in front of Bayden's face but got his hand swatted away. "She's all wrong for you, bro."

The three of them gawked at Angie as she walked away. I wasn't sure what she had that made them drool like horny teenage boys. I guess living in a small town made fresh meat enticing. Angie hadn't been here long, but she didn't seem too interested in dating, especially not my obnoxious brothers. I tossed back the rest of my drink; any other night, it would be one and done, but I had a rough day and my brothers are driving me crazy, so tonight would be a double down—down my throat.

"Why'd you cut out early today?" Quinn turned to look at me.

"You guys could handle it." Old Roy walked up with my brothers' beers. He owned the bar and could be anyone's grandfather with his white hair and watery blue eyes. He was a good guy, too—one whose colorful stories were a legend in this tight-knit community.

"Changing of the guard?" Quinn asked, glancing around at the lack of waiters and waitresses. Roy rarely ran drinks to tables unless he was the only one to do it, so the assumption was the next shift was clocking in.

Roy's deep voice was slow and measured. "Yep. Training a new waitress tonight." He left quickly as another table hailed him.

My brothers settled into their seats, and Bayden and Quinn took long pulls off their beers. Their mannerisms were identical, even though they weren't.

We often hung out here for drinks after work, which was why quitting time was my favorite part of the day. Usually, we'd haul ass over here and bullshit about everything and nothing. Tonight, I didn't feel much like talking.

"Who'd he sweet talk into working here?" Ethan scanned the bar.

I remained unfazed. As long as they could pull a beer and deliver it, who cared who Roy hired?

"What's wrong with working here?" Quinn asked defensively.

"Nothing, but—"

Quinn elbowed Ethan, "I'm messing with you. Lighten up. What's gotten into you guys today? You're all so damn glum." He didn't get much of a response, and with a sigh, he lifted his beer. "To Tuesday night."

A few tables down, Gypsy lifted her glass. "Are you boys being troublemakers again?" She wasn't one to blend in with her bright yellow and orange tie-dyed shirt. Her long gray hair hung loose to her waist in thick waves, and her bright-green eyes sparkled with mischief. Gypsy was a Woodstock leftover who never got the message that flower power and groovy were over decades ago.

"Yep, stirring things up as usual," Quinn lifted his mug in salute, spilling at least a sip over the edge.

Ethan's attention left his tablet, and he focused on the door. "Look who came to join the party."

Quinn ignored him, instead, continuing his conversation with Gypsy. Bayden glanced over his shoulder and stiffened. It was a Mom-walked-in-and-caught-you-in-the-candy-bowl kind of reaction.

Interesting.

Miranda—the new sheriff—stepped over the threshold. She pulled her hat off and nodded at Roy.

Bayden appeared to perk up, and I wondered if there was something between him and the sheriff. Bayden was Quinn's opposite in nearly every way, despite them being twins. His dark hair and sky-blue eyes weren't the only things that made him different. His close-lipped, quiet demeanor meant he kept things close to his vest. Given Ethan's words, I wasn't the only one who thought there might be something between our younger brother and the pretty new sheriff. Even though Angie had caught his eye earlier, it was obvious who had his full attention now.

Roy and Miranda shared a few words while I took in her five-foot six-ish frame. With her inky hair and almond-shaped eyes, she had an exotic air about her. Her fair skin didn't seem to soak up the sunshine like most of us, and her high cheekbones gave her a regal look.

While she appeared delicate, there was something fierce about her.

As if she read my mind, her dark gaze moved toward me then flicked to Bayden before returning to Roy.

Maybe there *was* something between them.

I took a swig of my beer and watched my brother study her.

"Don't make me show you a good time." Quinn's casual flirting with Gypsy brought a tittering laugh from the older woman.

"Boy, you wouldn't know what to do with me. Besides, you need some sweet thing who's your age." On the tail end of Gypsy's words, Angie walked to our table once more. Her brown eyes traced over every one of us, and we all leaned away from her except Bayden, who stayed focused on Miranda and didn't seem to notice Angie at all this time.

"Hey, boys." Angie paused.

Ethan was quick to speak up. "Hey, Angie, how are—"

"What's Benji doing here?" Bayden growled the words, and we all glanced in the door's direction. Benji, the local journalist for the Creekside Sentinel, stopped Miranda to talk to her, but she seemed less than thrilled.

"You know he likes to write stories on every new person in town, but Miranda's been dodging him like a pro." Quinn sounded proud of the sheriff.

Bayden turned and scowled, then lowered his beer to the table with a thump. There was definitely something going on with him and Miranda, if only in his mind for now. Was this flirtatious thing with Angie just a game? Was he trying to make the sheriff jealous?

Without a word about any of it, I finished my beer and signaled for another. Roy caught my eye and nodded before heading back to the bar.

The back of my neck prickled, and the air took on that electric charge that usually came right before a fight or a wicked storm. I smoothed my hand over my skin and took in the room. Nobody seemed like they were looking for a scuffle, and the last time I saw the sky, it was clear.

At the bar, a familiar-looking young woman smoothed her hands down the front of her apron with an unsure slowness. Her white-blonde hair framed her face and tumbled down her back. When she lifted her head, I jolted like someone had kicked me in the dangly bits.

Her brilliant, ocean-blue eyes locked on Roy with a hint of relief, and a smile crossed her full, cherry-red lips.

She said something I couldn't hear, and every bit of me tried to tune in to listen to her voice. Her fingertips brushed her cheekbone and shifted her hair back as she focused on Roy. Whatever he said had her nodding, and she gracefully tied her hair up with an elastic band she had wound around her wrist. Getting it up and out of her face only drew more attention to her beautiful features. She laughed at something Roy said, and the sweet lilting sound ribboned through me.

My heart stilled, then burst forth like it had been shocked with paddles—paddles covered in barbed wire that shredded me to bits.

What was Kandra doing here?

As I looked at my empty mug, I came face-to-face with the realization that she was the girl Roy mentioned.

"I know we are young, but I have never been more sure of anything in my life, Kandra." I got down on one knee and looked up at her, "Will you marry me?" She had tears rolling down her face, and I thought I was about to be the happiest man in the world. Then she said, "Noah, I love you, but I can't stay here in Cross Creek. I have dreams. I want to see the world, I want to be a photographer, and I can't do that if I'm here." Then, without so much as a second thought, she left, and I was there, kneeling like a chump and holding a ring I couldn't return.

"Noah?" The tone and inflection told me it wasn't the first time Quinn said my name.

"Yeah?" I locked down my emotions, hoping the shock didn't show on my face, but it was too late. He tapped both Ethan and Bayden to get their attention.

All eyes on him, he nodded toward the bar. "Is that..." Quinn seemed at a loss for words.

I looked at her again, hating every second of my life for the current moment. This was an awful dream—a nightmare—a cruel trick played by the powers that be. There was no way this could be happening. I refused to give in or let my brothers see how she still affected me.

Kandra laughed, her straight white teeth just as bright and perfect as they were back then.

Roy showed her the taps, and she filled a glass but didn't

tilt it as he taught her. The foamy head overflowed and spilled to the counter. She jumped back, and the glass slipped from her hand and shattered against the bar.

Her cheeks turned crimson, and a string of apologies fell from her lips.

My insides simmered, working up to a full boil. *Where are my apologies?*

Roy calmly helped her clean up the mess. The second attempt went better as she tipped the glass and triumph shone in her beautiful features.

"Is that Kandra?" Quinn finally found his voice.

"Damn." Ethan finished his beer and signaled Roy for another. "I'm not interested, but even I can see time has been kind to her. She's even more beautiful now." A *thunk* sounded under the table. "Ouch." He glared at Quinn. "What the—" Our brother must have kicked him.

"Don't even think about it," Quinn said to Ethan, before turning to me.

"Don't worry about it." Kandra and I were old news. She moved on when she realized I couldn't give her the life she wanted, so it didn't matter that she was back. Not one bit. "You can have her." I finished my beer.

"You can't have her," Quinn said to Ethan before turning to me. "Noah, you loved her, man. Maybe her coming back is a sign."

"Yeah, it's red, octagonal, and says *STOP* in big white letters." I glowered into my empty glass. I would not let Kandra back into my life. I swore back then I'd never hand anyone the tools to gut me ever again.

"Come on, Noah. Nobody's falling for it." Quinn's forgotten beer rested between his hands while he leaned across the table to get closer.

"There's nothing to fall for." I refused to look at her again for fear that something would give me away.

Quinn snorted. "You're still in love with her."

I shook my head. "Why don't you play matchmaker somewhere else? I'm not interested." I jerked my chin in Bayden's direction.

Quinn had to know he and Miranda were making eyes at each other, but Quinn ignored his twin and scrutinized me instead. "Nice try. You don't get to deflect this."

"There's nothing to deflect because there's nothing there." He didn't get it. Kandra and I were a dead end. There was nothing between us but bitter history, and no amount of probing, pestering, or pleading on his part could change that.

"Okay. Then you won't mind if I do this." Quinn stood up, cupped his hands around his mouth, and called out, "Another round, please."

"You're a dick." I wanted to kick him, but when I swung my boot, he stepped back.

He grinned. "I'm gonna hit the head."

Bayden stood up and moved in Angie's direction, but Ethan shoved him back into his chair. "Don't even think about it."

My brothers glared at each other.

"What's this sudden interest in Angie?" I asked.

Bayden looked from me to Ethan to Miranda. "Maybe I'm interested … or maybe I'm trying to make someone jealous."

"Which is it?" Ethan grumbled.

"What's it matter to you?"

"Sorry, guys." Roy dropped off our beers, ending the sibling exchange, and rushed away.

"Guess the universe is giving you a break since Roy

delivered the drinks." Ethan didn't take his eyes off Bayden. There was something feral and territorial in them. They were like two dogs going after the same bone.

I snorted. "A break? Yeah, right." Kandra didn't come to the table this time, but what about next time? What about tomorrow? There was no way I could avoid her forever. Unless she got fired, but even then, I'd probably just bump into her around town. If I was truly lucky, she would move away again.

Bayden stood up and walked toward Angie.

Ethan tried to grab him again, but he evaded capture.

"He's tenacious," I said.

Ethan turned to face me. "He's a pain in the ass." He took a drink of his beer. "You never told us why you cut out early today."

I was glad to steer the conversation in a direction that wasn't Kandra. "It's two years tomorrow." I didn't need to remind him, because he already knew.

He lifted his head. "You visit him?"

It was what I did. I sat down every year next to his granite headstone and talked to my dad.

"I should have known." Ethan sounded disappointed. "You know, you can talk to us."

We'd been over this before. "I know. Thank you."

"You don't have to suffer alone." The raw note in his voice said he was grieving too. Because I was the oldest and had more years with dad, I think I took it the hardest.

This time of the year was difficult for all of us, and we dealt with it in our own private ways.

I withdrew, Ethan pretended nothing happened, Bayden grew sullen, and Quinn ... well, I had no idea how he handled things because nothing ever seemed to faze him.

Though I knew it had devastated him, he seemed to have bounced back rather nicely.

"Thanks." I didn't know what else to say.

He seemed to sober up as he watched Bayden talk to Angie. "Two years," he muttered under his breath, more to himself than to me.

Time marched on as if our entire world hadn't been shaken to the core by the loss. Only two people had ever broken me; one couldn't help it, and the other was pulling beers at the taps. Seeing Kandra was an aftershock I didn't need today.

OTHER BOOKS BY KELLY COLLINS

Willow Bay

The Second Time Around

Here With You

Because You Said Yes

Cross Creek Novels

Broken Hart

Fearless Hart

Guarded Hart

Reckless Hart

JOIN MY READER'S CLUB AND GET A FREE BOOK.

Go to www.authorkellycollins.com

ABOUT THE AUTHOR

International bestselling author of more than thirty novels, Kelly Collins writes with the intention of keeping love alive. Always a romantic, she blends real-life events with her vivid imagination to create characters and stories that lovers of contemporary romance, new adult, and romantic suspense will return to again and again.

For More Information
www.authorkellycollins.com
kelly@authorkellycollins.com

Milton Keynes UK
Ingram Content Group UK Ltd.
UKHW020952311023
431661UK00016B/788